Also by Leon Garfield

Jack Holborn

Devil-in-the-Fog

Smith

Mister Corbett's Ghost

Black Jack

The Restless Ghost

The Restless Ghost

THREE STORIES
BY LEON GARFIELD

WITH ILLUSTRATIONS BY SAUL LAMBERT

PANTHEON BOOKS

1696131

To Madge and Peter

Contents

The Restless Ghost

PART ONE

D'you know the old church at Hove—the ruined one that lies three quarters of a mile back from the sea and lets the moon through like it was a church of black Nottingham lace?

Not an agreeable place, with its tumbledown church-yard brooded over by twelve elms and four threadbare yews which seem to be in mourning for better weather. A real disgrace to the Christian dead.

Twice a month the vicar used to come, preach briefly, and then be glad to get back to Preston. For he, no more than anyone, liked the villainous old crow of a sexton.

D'you remember the sexton? A hater of most things, but particularly of boys. A mean, shriveled, horny, sour, fist-shaking, and shouting old man, provoking much terror and a strong desire to set him down.

Some said the reason for his ill-temper was a grumbling belly; others said it was bunions (on account of his queer bounding limp when chasing off marauders and young hooters among his tombs); and others muttered that he was plagued by a ghost.

D'you remember the ghost? It was a drummer boy who used to drift through the churchyard on misty Saturday nights, glowing blue and green and drumming softly—to the unspeakable terror of all.

But that was twenty years ago. Then, two years after the haunting had begun, a certain band of smugglers had been caught and hanged—every last one of them in a dismal, dancing line—but not before they'd made a weird confession. The ghostly drummer had been no worse than a foundling lad, smeared with phosphorus to glow and gleam and scare off interruption while the smugglers followed darkly on. The churchyard had been their secret pathway to the safety of the Downs and beyond.

But that was eighteen years ago. The foundling lad had vanished and the smugglers had all moldered away. So why was the old sexton such a misery and violent against idly mischievous boys? What had they ever done to him (save hoot and squeak among his graves), that he should rush out and threaten them with his spade and an old musket that was no more use than a rotten branch?

An interesting question; and one that absorbed two pupils of Dr. Barron's school in Brighthelmstone to the exclusion of their proper studies. Dick Bostock and his dear friend, R. Harris.

"What say we scare the dying daylights out of him on Saturday night?" said Bostock to Harris the Wednesday before.

Harris, who was a physician's son and so interested in all things natural and supernatural, nodded his large head. Harris was thirteen and somewhat the more intellectual; but Bostock, though younger by a year, was the more wildly profound. Even separately, they were of consequence, but together they were a compendium of somber ingenuity and frantic daring.

So it was that, during three long and twilit walks to their separate homes, they hit upon a singularly eerie scheme.

And all the while, in his cottage by the lych gate, brooded the savage old sexton, unknowing that his angry days were numbered; and that two formidable pupils of Dr. Barron's had cast up their score.

"I'll give him something to moan about!" said Bostock, deeply.

"That you will," agreed Harris, with a gloomy admiration . . . for his part in the strange scheme was limited to fetching its wherewithal.

They met for the final time on the Saturday afternoon— as the light was dying—in an obscure lane that wound scarce two hundred yards to the north of the church.

They met in silence, as became their enterprise; but with nods and smiles, as became the success of it.

They walked for a little way till they came to a break in the hedge that led to a spot of some secrecy. There they unburdened themselves of their bundles.

"On a misty Saturday night," murmured Bostock, drawing out of his bundle a scarlet and black striped coat.

"There walked among the graves," whispered Harris, producing an old grenadier's cap.

"A fearful, ghostly drummer boy," said Bostock, bringing forth the necessary drum that rattled softly as he laid it in the long, stiff grass. He paused, then added, "Glowing?"

"Blue and green," nodded Harris, holding up a small stone pot, stolen from his father's laboratory.

In this was the phosphorescent paint—the eerie mixture of yellow phosphorus and pigmented ointment—furtively compounded by Harris from the recipe out of the condemned smugglers' confession.

Likewise, the apparel—borrowed off a brandy merchant whose son had gone for a soldier and not come back—was as the smugglers, dying, had declared. ("We dressed him as a grenadier, yer Honor. 'Twas all we had to hand.")

Hurriedly—for the day was almost gone—Dick Bostock put the garments on. As he did so, he felt a strange martial urge quicken his heart and run through his veins.

He took up the drum, slung it about his neck—and could scarce prevent himself from rolling and rattling upon it then and there.

Instead of which, watched by the silent Harris, he marched stiffly up and down as if possessed by the spirits of all the valorous youths who'd ever gone to war. Indeed, so brightly gleamed his eyes that he might well have done without the ghostly paint, but Harris, whose masterpiece it was, now offered it with a trembling hand.

"Now the sea mist's come, it'll not be dangerous," he murmured, shivering slightly as a heavy damp came drifting through the hedge.

"Dangerous?" said Bostock, scornfully.

"Moistness is necessary," said Harris, stroking the pot. "It takes fire or burns in dry air. But the mists will keep it damp . . ." Then, clutched with a sudden uneasiness, he muttered urgently, "Bostock! Don't be overlong!"

"Come, Harris! Open it up! Paint me, Harris. Make me

glow and gleam. I'll be but half an hour in the church-yard. More than enough to frighten that dismal pig out of his wits. Then I'll be back with you and safe and sound. I'll not outstay the mists—I promise you! Don't shake and shiver, Harris! D'you think I aim to stand among the tombs till I take fire and frizzle like a sausage?"

Harris continued to shiver; but even so, his more cautious soul was shamed before Bostock's valor . . . which appeared even more striking by reason of the grenadier's cap and drum.

He opened the pot. Then, as if there had been something within that had been sleeping—a monstrous glow-worm, maybe—there came slowly forth a pale, malignant gleaming . . .

Little by little, this uncanny light increased, shedding its queer radiance on the boys' peering faces, their stilled hands—and beyond them to the dense hawthorns that clustered about them, touching the tips of the twigs with the bright buds of a Devil's spring.

"Paint me, Harris," breathed Bostock, coldly afire.

So Harris, with a spatula stolen from his father's dispensary, began to smear the weird ointment onto the drummer's coat, his cuffs, his grenadier's cap, the fronts of his breeches, the tarnished cords of his drum, the drum-sticks, and—

"My face, Harris. Dab some on my face!"

"No—not there, Bostock! *Please*, not your face! There may be danger from it—"

"Then my hands, Harris. You must paint my hands!"

Once more, Harris was overcome. With spatula that shook so much that the evil substance spattered the grass with its chilly gleaming, he scraped what he could on the young skin of Bostock's hands.

The ointment felt unnaturally cold—even piercingly so. The heavy chill of it seemed to sink into the bones of his fingers and from thence to creep upward . . .

With a scowl of contempt at his own imagining, Bostock seized up the shining drumsticks—and brought them down on the drum with a sharp and formidable sound. Then again . . . and again, till the sticks quivered on the stretched skin as if in memory of the ominous rattle of war. He began to stalk to and fro . . .

Harris fell back, transfixed with a terrified admiration. Glowing green and blue, with bony rattle and a shadowy smile, there marched the ghostly drummer to the life. Or, rather, to the death.

"Am I fearful?" whispered Bostock, stopping the drumming and overcome with awe at the terror in his companion's eyes.

"Horrible, Bostock. Did I not know it was you, I'd drop down stone dead with fright."

"Do I walk like a ghost?" pursued Bostock.

Harris, who'd never viewed a ghost, considered it would need a pretty remarkable specter to come even within moaning distance of the grim and ghastly Bostock. He nodded.

"Then let's be gone," said Bostock, as hollowly as he might. "Watch from a distance, Harris. See without being seen."

Again, Harris nodded. Whereupon the phosphorescent drummer stalked eerily off, drumming as he went, toward the silent church.

The sea mists were now visiting among the elms of the churchyard, sometimes drifting out like bulky gray widows, for to peer at the inscription on some tumbled altar-tomb, before billowing off as if in search of another, dearer one . . .

The light from the sexton's cottage glimmered fitfully among the branches of one of the yews—for all the world as if the angry old man had at last given up human company and made his home in that dark, tangled place.

Bostock—watched by fascinated Harris from the churchyard's edge—smiled deeply, and stalked on.

Drum . . . drum . . . drum! he began; at first softly, then growing in rhythm and strength as if a grisly army was on its way.

Drum . . . drum . . . drum! The battalions are coming!
From where? From the mists and the shuddering tombs
platoons of long-dead grenadiers pricked up their bony
heads at the call of the old drum, grinned, nodded—
moved to arms . . .

Or so it seemed to the phosphorescent Bostock as he
trundled back and forth, uneasily enjoying himself and
awaiting the sexton's terror.

Now the sound of his drum seemed to echo—doubtless
by reason of the confining mists. He must remember to
ask Harris about it. Harris knew of such things. Also, the
banking vapors tended to reflect, here and there, his own
phosphorescence, as if in a foul and filthy mirror.

Sea mists were queer, especially at night. Nonetheless,
their heavy damp eased the tingling on his hands by confining the power of the malevolent ointment.

There was no sign yet of the sexton. Was it possible he
hadn't heard the drum? Could the horrible old man have
gone deaf? With a touch of irritation, Bostock began to
drum more loudly, and stalked among the tombs that lay
closest to the cottage.

He hoped the mists and elms had not quite swallowed
him up from Harris's view. After all, he'd no wish to per-
form for the night and the dead alone (supposing the
sexton never came). Harris ought to get some benefit.

Besides which, a most gloomy loneliness was come upon him. A melancholy loneliness, the like of which he'd never known.

"Harris!" he called softly, but was too far off to be heard by the physician's son.

Suddenly, he must have passed into a curious nestling of mists. The echo of his drum seemed to have become more distinct. Strange effect of nature. Harris would be interested.

"Harris—"

There seemed to be layers in the mist . . . first soft and tumbled, then smooth—

These smooth patches he fancied he glimpsed through shifting holes. Or believed he did. For once more he seemed to be reflected in them—then lost from sight—then back again . . . glowing briefly blue and green . . .

"Harris—"

Now the reflected image stayed longer. Marched with him . . . drummed with him . . .

Yet in that mirror made of mist, there was a strange deception. Though no ointment had been applied to Bostock's face, this other drummer's narrow brow and sunken cheeks were glowing with—

"*Harris!*"

But Harris never heard him. Harris, most precipitantly, had fled. Harris, from his watching place beyond the graves, had already seen it. He had observed that his gleaming friend had attracted a companion. Another, palely glowing grenadier!

"Harris—Harris—" moaned the painted Bostock as the terrible drummer paused and stared at him with eyes that were no eyes but patches of blackness in a tragic, moldered face.

Suddenly, the boy recovered the use of his legs; or rather, his legs recovered the use of the stupefied boy. And wrenched him violently away.

In truth, he did not know he'd begun to run, till running he'd been for seconds. Like a wounded firefly, he twittered and stumbled and wove wildly among the graves. All his frantic daring was now abruptly changed into its reverse. Frantic terror engulfed him—and was doubled each time he looked back.

The phantom drummer was following . . . drumming as it came . . . staring as if with crumbling reproach for the living boy's mockery of its unhappy state.

Now out of the churchyard fled the boy, much hampered by his ridiculous costume and overlarge drum, that thumped as his knees struck it—like a huge, hollow heart.

Into the lane whence he'd come, he rushed. He might have been a craven soldier, flying some scene of battle, with his spectral conscience in pursuit.

At the end of the lane, he paused, groaned "Harris!"

miserably once more. But no Harris answered—only the drum . . . drum . . . drum! of the phantom he'd drawn in his wake.

Very striking was its aspect now, as it drifted out of the shadows of the lane. Its clothing was threadbare—and worse. Its cap was on the large size . . . as were its cuffs that hung upon the ends of its bone-thin fingers like strange, frayed mouths.

And on its face was a look of glaring sadness, most somber to behold.

Not that Bostock was much inclined to behold it, or to make its closer acquaintance in any way.

Yet even though he'd turned and fled, trembling on, the tragic drummer's face remained printed on his inward eye . . .

"I'm going home—going home!" sobbed Bostock as he ran. "You can't come with me there!"

But the sound of the drum grew no fainter . . . and the specter followed on.

"What d'you want with me? What have I done? I'm Dick Bostock—and nought to you! Dick Bostock, d'you hear? A stranger—no more!"

Drum . . . drum . . . drum! came on behind him; and when the boy helplessly turned, he saw on the phantom's face a look of unearthly hope!

"This is my home!" sobbed the boy at last, when he

came to the comfortable little road he knew so well. "Leave me now!"

He stumbled down the row of stout flint cottages till he came to his own. With shaking fingers, he unlatched his garden gate.

"Leave me! Leave me!"

Drum . . . drum . . . drum! came relentless down the street.

"Now I'm safe—now I'm safe!" moaned Bostock, for he'd come to the back of his house.

There, under the roof, was his bedroom window, in which a candle warmly burned.

"Thank God!" whispered Bostock of a sudden: the terrible drumming had stopped.

He drew in his breath, prayed—and looked behind him.

"Thank God!" he whispered again: the phantom was gone.

Now he turned again to his window and hastened to climb up an old apple tree that had ever served him for stairs. He reached the longed-for window. He looked within. He gave a groan of terror and dismay.

In *his* room, seated on *his* bed, looking out of *his* window—was the spectral drummer once more!

And, as the living boy stared palely in, so the dead one stared out . . . then, it lifted up its arm and pointed.

It pointed unmistakably past the unhappy Bostock . . . over his shoulder and toward the churchyard whence it had come.

There was no doubt of its meaning. None at all. The boy was now condemned to fill the place left vacant by the usurping ghost.

Never was a live boy worse situated. Never had an apple tree borne whiter fruit . . . that now dropped down, dismally phosphorescent, to the cold, damp ground.

PART TWO

The miserable Bostock, phosphorescent as ever, stood forlornly under the apple tree. The phantom had caught him and trapped him most malevolently.

To appear as he was, at his own front door, was more than his courage or compassion allowed.

His father and mother. Their fury on his awesome appearance, he could have endured. But there was worse than that. Would they not have died of fright when they faced his usurper—the grim inhabitant of his room—that other shining drummer boy?

Tears of misery and despair stood in his eyes, ran over

and fell upon his hands—thereby easing the tingling to which they'd become subject.

Harris! He must go to Harris, the physician's large-headed son. Wise old Harris . . .

He crept out into the road and ran deviously to a prosperous house that stood on the corner. Candles shone in the parlor window. The good doctor and his lady were sat on either side of their fire. Harris was not among them. Somewhat eerily, Bostock flitted to the back of the house. Harris's bedroom was aglow. He had returned.

"Harris!" called Bostock, urgently. But Harris's window was tight shut, against the damp air . . . and more.

"Harris! For pity's sake, Harris!"

No answer. Harris had heard nothing save, most likely, the uneasy pounding of his own heart.

Desperately, Bostock cast about for pebbles to fling at the window. With no success. What then? The drum! He would tap on the drum. Harris would hear that. For certain sure, Harris would hear that.

And Harris did hear it. Came to his window aghast. Ever of a studious, pimplish disposition, his spots burned now like little fiery mountains in the ashes of his face. Not knowing which drummer he was beholding, he took it for the worse. Bostock would have shouted; Bostock would have thrown pebbles at the window . . . not beaten the evil drum!

He vanished from his window with a soundless cry of dismay. His curtain was drawn rapidly and Bostock—faintly shining Bostock—was left, rejected of the living.

So he began to walk, choosing the loneliest, darkest ways. Twice he frightened murmuring lovers, winding softly home. But he got no pleasure from it . . .

Glumly, he wondered if this was a sign of slipping into true ghostliness. For it wasn't to be supposed that graveyard phantoms—unlike daring boys—delighted in being terrible. Most likely, they were pained by the horror they inspired . . .

This mournful thought led to another, even sadder. He wondered if the phantom in his bedroom was now losing its weird glow, and generally filling out into a perfect semblance of the boy whose place it had stolen.

Very likely. Nature and un-nature, so to speak, were disagreeably tidy. They cared for nothing left over. Vague and confused memories of Dr. Barron's sleep-provoking voice filled his head . . . and most earnestly he wished he'd attended more. He felt the lack of any solid learning from which he might have found an answer to his plight.

Ghosts, phantoms, unquiet spirits of all denominations stalked the earth for a purpose. And until that purpose was achieved, they were doomed to continue in their melancholy office.

This much, Bostock had a grasp of: but beyond it,

nothing. If ever Dr. Barron had let fall anything that might have been of help, Bostock could not remember it. Neither tag nor notion nor fleeting word remained in his head. He was alone and shining—and his hands were beginning to burn.

Of a sudden, he found himself in the lane that wound to the north of the church. Back to the churchyard he was being driven, by forces outside of his reckoning.

"Goodbye, Harris," he whispered, as he stumbled through the broken hedge and across the grass toward the night-pierced bulk of the ruined church. "Goodbye forever."

The thick grass muttered against his legs and his drum grumbled softly under his lifting knees.

"Goodbye, light of day; goodbye Dr. Barron; goodbye my mother and father; goodbye my friends and enemies; goodbye my cat Jupiter and my dear mice . . . Oh Harris, Harris! Remember me! Remember your young friend Bostock—who went for a ghost and never came back!"

And then the evil thought returned that the specter would have become another Bostock. Harris would have no cause to remember what Harris would never know had gone.

On which Bostock felt a pang of bitterness and anger; but it vanished when he found himself among the elms. He sadly surveyed his future realm.

There lay the graves, all leaning and tumbled like stone ships, frozen in a stormy black sea. The mists were almost gone and the starlight glimmered coldly down. What was he to do? How best discharge his new office? The drum. Beat the drum and drift uncannily to and fro.

So he began, drum . . . drum . . . drum! But, it must be admitted, he tended to stumble rather than to drift, for where a phantom might have floated, Bostock trod. Many a time he caught his bruised feet in roots that were more uncanny than he. But there was yet something more frightening than that. His hands were burning more and more.

He tried to subdue the pain by thinking on other things. But what thoughts could come to a boy in a dark church-yard save unwelcome ones?

He gave several dismal groans, more pitiful even than a wandering spirit might have uttered. His poor hands were afire . . .

Water—he must have water! He felt in the long grass for such damp as the mists might have left behind. Too little . . . too little. He ran from grave to grave, laying his hands against the cold, moist stone. To no purpose. He looked to the ragged, broken church . . . Of a sudden, a hope plucked at his heart.

There was to be a christening on the morrow. Already, it had been delayed for two months on account of a chill.

A fisherman's child . . . Harris—interested in all such matters—had sagely talked of it. ("In my opinion, they ought to wait another month. But there's no arguing with superstitious fisherfolk! They'll douse the brat on Sunday, come snivel, come sneeze, come galloping decline!")

The font! Maybe it was already filled?

Bostock began to run. Frantic sight. His luminous knees thumped the underside of the drum, setting up the rapid thunder of an advance. His luminous sleeves, his gleaming cuffs with his distracted hands held high, flared through the night like shining banners. And, as he passed them by, the old cracked tombs seemed to gape in amazement—and lean as if to follow.

At last, he reached the church, halted, briefly prayed, and crept inside.

All was gloom and deep shadows, and the passage of night air through rents in the stone caused the untenanted pews to creak and sigh, as if under the memory of generations of Sunday sleepers . . .

Bostock approached the font. Thank God for Christian fisherfolk! It was filled.

With huge relief, he sank his wretched, shining hands into the icy water. Uncanny christening. They glimmered against the stone beneath the water like nightmarish fish . . . But oh! the blessed stoppage of the pain!

He stood, staring toward the altar, upon which, from a

superior hole in the roof, such light as was in the night sky dropped gently down.

He started, and in so doing scraped the drum against the font. It rattled softly through the dark.

What had made him start? He was not alone in the church. A figure was crouched upon the altar step. A figure seemingly sunk in sleep or prayer or stony brooding . . .

On the sound of the drum, the figure turned—and groaned to its feet.

It was the sour and savage old sexton. Bitter moment for Bostock. Too late now to get any joy out of frightening the old man stupid. Bostock, his hands in the font, was more frightened by far. Unhappily, he awaited the old man's wrath.

But the old man only stood and stared at him. There was no rage in his withered face; only wonderment and fear. Nor was it a sudden fear, such as a man might betray on first seeing a ghost. It was the deep, abiding fear of a man to whom a ghost came often—to plague him on misty Saturday nights. For in the shadows of the church, he took the glimmering Bostock to be that phantom that had troubled him this many a long year. Yet . . . with a difference—

"Into the church?" he whispered. "Even into the church,

now? What does it mean? You never came in the church before. Is it—is it forgiveness, at last?"

Bostock stared at the shriveled old sexton—that terror of marauding boys. Very miserable and desolate was the ancient wretch. Very pitiful was the hope in his eyes—

"Yes!" cried the sexton, with misguided joy. "It's forgiveness! I see it in your eyes! Pity! Blessed, blessed pity!"

Fearful to speak, or even to move, Bostock gazed at the old man who now hobbled toward him. There was a look of tarnished radiance on his face as secrets long knotted in his heart began to unravel and give him peace.

"At last my treasure, dear spirit! Now I can go to it! It's all right now? In this holy place, you've come to forgive? My treasure! All these years of waiting for it! All these years of misery . . . all these years of longing . . . How many? Eighteen! But all's forgiven now . . . At last, at last!"

Careless of the raging ointment, Bostock drew his hands out of the font as the old man tottered by, mumbling and gabbling as he went.

For the old man did pass him by, his face quite transfigured by yearning and relief. He went out into the tumbledown churchyard, clucking over the neglected graves like an ancient gardener, revisiting an overgrown garden he'd once tended well . . .

Absorbed beyond measure, the luminous Bostock followed—straining to catch the drift of the old man's broken words.

There was no doubt now that the ghost had been that of the foundling boy who'd long ago drummed for the smugglers. Likewise, there was no doubt that the sexton had brought him to his death.

"I never knew you was ailing, my dear. I never knew the paint was a-poisoning you. I swear I'd never have made you go out when the mists was gone if I'd known! Ask the others—if you're situated to do so. They'll tell you I never knew. Thought you was pretending for more of the haul. Thought your cries and moans were play acting. Never, never thought you'd die, my dear!"

Thus he mumbled and muttered—half over his shoulder—to what he fancied was the ghost he hoped had forgiven him at last.

For it turned out that this ancient sexton had been of the smugglers himself, and had most cunningly escaped hanging with the rest.

"There, my dear. There's your grave. See—I've tended it all these years . . ."

He paused by a patch of ground where the grass had been newly cut.

"But my treasure . . . now I can go fetch my treasure. Now I can live once more . . . now I can leave this accursed place! A—a house in London, maybe . . . a coach and pair . . . Just for my last years . . . my treasure will make up for all!"

Hastening now, he fumbled among the altar-tombs, heaving at the slabs till at last he came upon the one he sought.

"It's here! It's here!"

With a loud grinding, the slab of stone slid sideways and fell upon the ground. The old man reached within and fumbled for the hoard that had waited in the earth for eighteen years.

Bostock moved nearer. He strained to see. He sniffed the heavy air. His heart contracted in grief for the luckless sexton.

From the smugglers' hiding place came forth only the dismal smell of rotting tea and moldered tobacco leaf. All had crumbled away.

The old man had begun to sob. A ruinous sound.

Quite consumed with pity, Bostock laid a hand on the sexton's wasted shoulder and muttered, "I'm sorry . . . truly sorry, sir . . ."

Whereupon the old man whirled round upon him in a sudden access of amazement and fist-shaking rage.

The hand on his shoulder, the voice in his ear had been no ghost's, but those of a mortal boy.

He beheld the fantastic Bostock. An undersized, some-

what timid grenadier whose protruding ears alone pre-
vented his mansize cap from quite extinguishing him.

Was it to this small, mocking villain he'd opened his
heart and betrayed it?

He stared—but saw no laughter in Bostock's face.
Rather did he see a startled compassion that came in a
gentle flood from Bostock's heart and filled up Bostock's
eyes—making them to shine softly—and from thence,
ran resistless down Bostock's cheeks. The boy was crying
for him. The boy had partly understood, and was grieving
for the wastage of his poor life, for his heart that had
turned to dust—by reason of the haunting of his soul.

"What—what are you doing here, boy?"

Bostock shook his head, made to wipe his eyes, then
stared, frightened, at his luminous hand and hid it behind
his back.

On which the sexton went gray with horror—on the
memory of an old, old occasion. He gave some four or
five harsh, constricted cries—for all the world as if the
organ that produced them was stirring after long disuse.
Then he partly screamed and partly shouted, "What
have you done with your hands? What—have—you—
done? Oh God, you'll die! You'll die again! *He* died of it!
A doctor! Quick—quick! This time, I'll save you! please
God, let me save you this time!"

He reached out and seized the terrified Bostock by a

cuff. Now he began to drag him, as fast as his hobble would permit, out of the churchyard and toward Brighthelmstone. And all the while, he panted, "Let me save him—let me save him!"

Tremendous sight . . . remarked on for years afterward by startled tavern-leavers who'd glimpsed the bounding, limping old man and the phosphorescent boy.

A sight never to be forgotten—least of all by Dr. Harris at whose door the sexton banged and kicked till it was opened.

Before he could be gainsaid, he'd dragged the wretched Bostock in and begged the doctor try to save him.

"What's amiss? What's amiss, then?"

"He'll die—he'll die!" wept the sexton. "Just like the other one!"

Then out tumbled the sexton's grim secret while the doctor's household listened in judgment and in pity. For though the old man had been a murderer—had done in the foundling by his eager greed—it was plain to all he'd paid a high price for his crime.

"This boy will be saved," muttered Dr. Harris, washing the evil ointment away and staring at the inflamed skin beneath. "But may God forgive you for that other one."

Now it seemed to Bostock as he sat, with wise old nightgowned Harris come down to be by his side, that the night was grown suddenly warmer. The fire burned bright—as if an obstruction had been lifted off the chimney . . .

He was not alone in noticing this. It was remarked on by the doctor, who diagnosed a sudden, beneficial draft. Likewise, it was observed by the sexton—the confessed murderer—who peered about, then glanced toward the window as if the cause was passing down the street. For he nodded . . .

And though Bostock, who followed his gaze, saw nothing but darkness, he knew that the usurping phantom had at last slipped away, its purpose achieved, its office at full term.

So did the phantom drummer boy haunt the churchyard no more? Did it never stalk on misty Saturday nights? And was its drum heard never again to echo across the tumbled tombs? Yes: but only once more.

The sexton was put in prison against the day of his trial. But he never lived for the hanging that would have been his fate. He died a week before his earthly judgment, and so was able to be buried in consecrated ground. His own churchyard.

D'you remember when they buried the old sexton at Hove? It was late on a Saturday night, and the sea mists were coming up.

D'you remember the sound of drumming that accom-

panied his coffin? And the gentle beating as it was low-
ered into its grave? It had a strangely forgiving sound . . .
They say it was a retreat that was being beaten, but to
Bostock and Harris it sounded more like a welcome—
welcome home.

Vaarlem and Tripp

It's certain he has a great gift: but otherwise he is a very contemptible, vile little man—strong-smelling, even, and well-known in the Amsterdam courts for fraud, embezzlement, and bankruptcy. It's very humiliating to be his pupil, but as my father says, if God has planted a lily in a cesspool, one must stop up one's nose and go down. Of late, my task has been to choose his brushes, pigment, and canvas. He tells me this is as important a part of the craft of painting as there is, but the truth of the matter is that he's so much in debt and disgrace that he daren't show his face outside the studio. My name is Roger Vaarlem; my master is Joseph Tripp, of course.

A month ago he was before the Burghers, who told him his portrait of the Admiral was unacceptable—insulting, even—and demanded their advance of guilders back. Having spent it, he offered to paint the Admiral again, but was not trusted—and rightly. Truth to Nature was one thing (no one could deny the portrait had a deal of truth in it, for my master has his gift), but truth to one's country and employers must come first. So he was given the opportunity of redeeming himself by painting a grand battlepiece to be hung in the Town Hall. Or prosecution in the courts again. Angrily (he told me) he accepted and was granted a cabin aboard the *Little Willem*. We sailed at half past eight this morning.

Though the early morning had been warm and brilliant, he was muffled in every garment he could find, careless of their cleanliness which is a strong point aboard Dutch ships. It was very shameful to be walking along beside him, carrying his sketchbooks and other belongings which smelled worse than the tar and pickled fish with which the air was strong. There were two ships of ninety guns nodding in a stately fashion upon the gentle tide: cathedrals of gilded wood with triple spires and delicate crosses, netted and festooned as for a Saint's Day. The thought crossed my mind of parting from Mynheer Tripp and going to sea on my own, but my father would have prosecuted him for negligence and fraud and he'd have gone to jail for it.

Then we came to the *Little Willem* and he at once began to complain that it was insufficiently armed and pointed out the maze of stitching on the fore topsail where English musketfire had peppered it to a sieve. Together with all his other qualities, he is a great coward, and I felt myself blush as he ranted on in the hearing of one of the ship's officers. Then, with my hand to his elbow, he went aboard, stepping down on the deck as if it were a single floating plank and not secure.

The *Little Willem*, being but a smallish barquentine, could offer only a tiny cabin next to the surgeon's, but at least it was clean, which flattered Mynheer Tripp unwarrantably.

"Go away, Vaarlem!" he mumbled, and crawled onto the bunk—for the motion of the ship at its moorings was already unsettling his stomach. So I left him and went out onto the main deck in the sunny air and watched the crew go about their business in the rigging and on the yards.

"How come a fine-looking lad like you goes about with an old ragbag like him?"

Mynheer Leyden—an officer of good family—was standing by me.

I answered, "Sir—he's a great man, whatever you may

think, and will be remembered long after you and me are forgot."

After all, one has one's pride!

Mynheer Leyden would have answered, but Captain Kuyper began shouting from the quarter-deck to cast off and Mynheer Leyden shrugged his smooth shoulders and went about his duties. These seemed to consist in putting his hands behind his back and pacing the larboard rail, nodding to the crowd of fishwives and early clerks who always throng the harbor in the mornings to watch the glorious ships heave and puff out their sails like proud white chests and lean their way into the dangerous sea.

Once out of the harbor, the foresail was set and I went below to inform Mynheer Tripp he was missing a very wonderful sight, for there was not much wind and the great spread of canvas seemed to be but breathing against invisible, creaking stays. But he was already up and about —and in a more cheerful mood. He'd had intelligence that the *Little Willem* was to sail west by southwest to lure enemy vessels into pursuit, when they'd be blown out of the water by our own great ships which would be following on the next tide. His cheerfulness arose from the discovery that the *Little Willem* was the swiftest vessel in the Channel and was not intended to fight.

"A clean pair of heels, eh? Ha-ha!" he kept saying . . .

and grinning in a very unwholesome manner. It was the only time I'd ever known him take a real pleasure in cleanliness. Later on, his spirits rose high enough for him to behave in his usual way. He began soliciting guilders from the officers to portray them prominently in the battle-piece. Full of shame—for he was earning a good deal of contempt—I warned him he'd be prosecuted for false pretenses.

"Why?" he muttered angrily—the wind catching the soft brim of his black hat and smacking his face with it.

"Because they won't be larger than thumbnails, sir!"

"You mind your own business, Vaarlem!" he snarled, quite beside himself where guilders were concerned. "If those little tinsel nobodies tell their dough-faced relatives that such and such a blob of paint is their darling—well? Why not? What's wrong with a little family pride? Immortal, that's what they'll be! So keep your middle-class nose out of my affairs, Master Vaarlem . . . or I'll paint you as an Englishman!"

He stalked away, holding his hat with one hand and his filthy shawls and oil-stained coat with the other. But soon after, he sidled back again and remarked ingratiat-ingly, "No need to tell your papa everything I say, Roger, dear lad . . . Words spoke in haste . . . no need for mis-understandings, eh? Dear boy . . ."

He was so mean, he was frightened my father would withdraw me as his pupil—and with me would go guilders. I looked at him coldly, while he bit his lip and brooded uneasily on whether he'd cut off his nose to spite his face—not that either woud have been the loser.

I was more offended than I cared to let him know, so I obliged by keeping my nose out of his affairs for the remainder of the day. Which wasn't difficult, as he kept to the Great Cabin with the surgeon. Not that he was really ill—God forbid!—but he was cunningly picking the surgeon's wits relative to every ache and pain that plagued him. While all the while, the simple surgeon was happily imagining himself in the forefront of the Town Hall's battlepiece, a hero forever. (Mynheer Tripp did indeed make a small sketch of him: a very wonderful piece of work—for somehow he'd caught a look of bewilderment and embarrassment in the surgeon's eyes as if God had too often stared them out.)

I'd intended to leave him for much longer than I did: at one time in the day I'd very serious thoughts indeed of leaving him altogether and fighting for Holland. This was when we saw our first English sail and there was great activity on the lower gun deck against the chance of an encounter. She was a handsome, warlike vessel, bosoming strongly along. "A seventy-four," remarked Mynheer Leyden briskly. "By tomorrow she'll be driftwood!" Then

we outpaced her and the sea was as clean as a German
silver tray.

It was a few minutes before half past eight o'clock in
the evening. I'd been on deck together with several officers. The wind was gone. The air was still. A sharp-edged
quarter moon seemed to have sliced the clouds into strips,
so that they fell away slowly, leaving dark threads behind.
Earlier, Mynheer Leyden had been urging me to speak
with the Captain about my becoming a midshipman, for
I was of good family and too good for Mynheer Tripp.
To be a painter was a lower-class ambition. ("All right!
He has his gift! But what's that to you and me? God gave
him sharp eyes—but He gave us good families! Vaarlem,
my boy—I can't make you out!") Then, a few minutes
before half past eight, Mynheer Leyden said quietly,
"Vaarlem, you'd best go down and fetch him." Which
I did.

"Sir, you must come up on deck at once."

Mynheer Tripp glanced at me irritably, began to
mumble something, then thought better of it. He stood
up and wrapped himself in the filthy shawls and coat he'd
strewn about the cabin.

"Hurry, sir!"

"Why? The sea won't run away . . . and if it does,
I shan't be sorry!" He followed me onto the deck.

"Look, Mynheer Tripp! The Englishman!"

For a proud moment, I thought he'd had enough brandy to make him behave like a Dutchman, for he stood quite still and silent. Then the brandy's effect wore off and his own miserable spirit shone through. Every scrap of color went from his face and he began to tremble with terror and rage!

"Madman!" he shrieked—and I wished myself at the bottom of the sea and Mynheer Tripp with me. The Englishman was within half a kilometer and still moving softly toward us, pulled by two longboats whose oars pricked little silver buds in the moonswept sea. She was as silent as the grave, and any moment now would turn broadside on and greet us with the roar of thirty-seven iron mouths. For she was the seventy-four.

Mynheer Tripp seized my arm and began dragging me toward the quarter-deck, shouting outrageously, "Move off! For God's sake move off! We'll all be killed! How dare you do such a thing! Look! Look! This boy . . . of a good family . . . very important! If he's harmed I'll be prosecuted by his father. And so will you! I demand to go back! For Vaarlem's sake! Oh my God! A battle!"

They must have heard him aboard the Englishman. I could only pray that no one aboard it knew Dutch! I felt myself go as red as a poppy. To be used by this villainous coward as a mean excuse—I all but fought with him!

"You pig, Mynheer Tripp!" I panted. "This time you've gone too far!"

"Pig?" he hissed, between roarings at the Captain. "You shut your middle-class mouth, Master Vaarlem! These noodles have no right to expose me—us to such danger! I'll sue—that's what I'll do! In the courts!"

Captain Kuyper—a man who'd faced death a hundred times and now faced it for maybe the last—stared at Mynheer Tripp as if from a great distance.

"You are perfectly right, sir. This ship is no place for you. You will be put off in the boat and rowed to where you may observe the engagement in safety. Or go to Holland. Or go to Hell, sir! As for the boy—he may stay if he chooses. I would not be ashamed to die in *his* company."

To my astonishment, before I could answer—and God knows what I'd have said—Mynheer Tripp burst out with, "How dare you, sir, put such ideas into a boy's head! What d'you expect him to say? A boy of good family like him! Unfair, sir! Cruel! Dishonest! What can he know? I warn you, if you don't put him off, I'll not stir from your miserable ship! Both of us—or none! Oh, there'll be trouble! In the courts!"

Then he turned his mean, inflamed face toward me and muttered urgently, "Keep quiet, Vaarlem! None of your business! Don't you dare say a word! I forbid it!"

Captain Kuyper shrugged his shoulders and turned away. "Put them both in the boat, and let one man go with them to take the oars. Immediately! I want Mynheer Tripp off this ship at once. Or by God, I'll throw him off!"

Quite sick with shame, I followed Mynheer Tripp, who'd scuttled to the boat and hopped into it, clutching his sketchbooks and horrible clothes about him—in a panic that the Captain would do him a mischief.

The sailor who rowed us was a tall, silent fellow by the name of Krebs. For about twenty minutes he said nothing, but rowed with a seemingly slow though steady stroke. Mynheer Tripp, his head hunched into his shoulders, grasped my wrist and stared at the diminishing bulk of the *Little Willem* which lay between us and the huge Englishman. Implacably, the Englishman came nearer and nearer and still did not turn. We could no more see the longboats . . . but the men in them must have had nerves of iron, for they were within musket range of the *Little Willem* and could have been shot to pieces.

"Faster! Faster!" urged my master, as the bowsprit of the Englishman appeared to nod above the *Willem*'s deck. There looked to be no more than fifty meters between them. Then she began to slew round . . . ponderously . . . malignantly . . .

"Will you watch from here, sirs?" Krebs had stopped rowing. There was nothing contemptuous in the way he spoke. He simply wanted to know.

"Is it—is it safe?"

Krebs eyed the distance. "Most likely—yes, sir."

The two ships now lay side by side—the Englishman's aft projecting beyond the *Willem*. Her aftercastle, much gilded and gleaming under three lanterns, rose nearly as high as the *Willem*'s mizzenyard. A very unequal encounter. Perhaps she thought so? And was waiting for a surrender?

Krebs shipped his oars and stuck his chin in his great hands. Calmly he stared at the dark shape of his own ship, outlined against the somber, spiky brown of her enemy. Though the shrouds and yards must have been alive with marksmen, nothing stirred to betray them.

"Thank God we ain't aboard!" he remarked at length. Mynheer Tripp nodded vigorously. He'd begun to make sketches by the light of a small lantern. Approvingly, Krebs glanced at them. Very workmanlike. I began to feel cold and lonely. Was I the only one who wished himself back aboard the *Little Willem*?

The beginnings of a breeze. The great, ghostly sails of the Englishman began to shift, but not quite to fill. The *Willem*'s sail, being smaller, bellied out more fatly. The bold little Dutchman and the skinny Englishman began to move. Masts, which had seemed all of one ship, began to divide—to part asunder . . .

There seemed to be a moment of extraordinary stillness —even breathlessness—when suddenly a huge yellow flower of fire grew out of the side of the Englishman. (Beautiful Dutch lady—take my murdering bouquet!)

And then enormous billows of reddish smoke roared and blossomed up, blundering through the rigging and fouling the sails and sky. The engagement was begun.

A faint sound of screaming and shouting reached us, but was instantly drowned in the roar of the *Willem*'s broadside. Then the Englishman fired again—this time with grapeshot, which makes an amazing, shrieking sound as it flies.

"The mainmast! D'you see? They've got the mainmast!" muttered Krebs, his face white even in the reddish glare of the encounter. "Shrouds and halyards cut through— murder for them on deck! Slices them in two and three parts! Murder, it is!"

The *Willem* was still firing—but not full broadsides. Half her ports must have been shattered.

"They've got to heave the dead out of the way!" Krebs said very urgently—as if it was his immediate task. "Can't get to the powder quick enough with all them dead tangling up the trunnions . . . got to heave 'em out . . .

Cap'n'll be down there now—he'll be doing the right thing—"

Another flash and roar from the Englishman: not so vast as the first. Was she disabled, too?

"Quarter-deck cannon," mumbled Krebs, suddenly scowling. "Now you'll see—" Again she roared. "Upper deck cannon . . . fourteen killers there!" A third blaze and roar. Krebs nodded. "Lower deck. They know what they're at. Give no chance . . . no chance at all . . ."

The *Willem* seemed to have stopped firing. "Look! Poor devils up in the crosstrees. D'ye see? Firebrands! Nought else left! But they'll never reach to the Englishman. Poor devils! Oh, God! She's afire herself! Keep your heads down, sirs! She'll be going up in a minute! A—ah!"

Even as he spoke, the fire must have reached the *Willem*'s powder store. There was a glare and a thunderous crackling sound like the end of the world—as indeed for many it was. With a shriek of terror, Mynheer Tripp —who'd been extraordinarily absorbed throughout the encounter, oblivious to everything but his rapid, intent drawing—flung himself to the bottom of the boat: a quaking bundle of disgusting rags. Then the great light went out of the sky and the air was full of smoke and the sharp, bitter smell of spent powder and burnt-out lives. Pieces of wood began to kiss the water about us. When at last the smoke drifted up to the moon, we saw the

guilty hump of the Englishman sliding away, leaving nothing more behind than a torn-up patch of sea, rough with driftwood and darknesses.

"Oh, God! Now what's to become of us?" wept Mynheer Tripp. I begged him to be quiet, for things were bad enough without his assistance. Krebs had been hit in the neck by a flying piece of iron and was bleeding like a pig. If he wasn't bandaged, he'd die. Mynheer Tripp plucked at one of his shawls—not offering it, but indicating that, if pressed, he'd part with it. It was filthy enough to have killed Krebs outright: by poisoning. There was nothing for it but to use my shirt; which I did, watched by Mynheer Tripp, who snarled when I tore it into strips, "I hope you know that was your best linen, Vaarlem!"

Which mean remark did nothing but gain me unnecessary thanks from Krebs, who could scarcely speak: his wound having severed a tendon and opened a great vessel. He lay in the bottom of the boat while I took the oars, watched by that dirty jelly in the stern. All I could see of Mynheer Tripp were his miserably reproachful eyes.

"You'll die of cold," he mumbled furiously.

"I can keep warm by rowing, sir!" I said, hoping to shame him. I pulled toward the *Little Willem*'s grave in the frail hope of survivors, but found none. Then, under Krebs's whispered directions, I began to row eastward, into the path of our hoped-for followers on the coming tide. But, being no craftsman of oars, we did little more than drift in that dark and hostile sea: Mynheer Tripp, Krebs, and I. For two or even three hours . . . As Mynheer Tripp had predicted, it was violently cold. I began to shiver and sweat at the same time. My hands were growing very sore and swollen. When I paused to shift my grip, I found them to be bleeding; and Mynheer Tripp, without once stopping, moaned and cursed the sea and the murdering Englishman. Which served no purpose at all. But then he's not the best of companions in such circumstances. He hates the sea and can't abide the sight of blood. Also, there are a million other things capable of panicking him. The chief problem is to avoid being infected by this.

At about one o'clock the breeze began to blow more briskly and in a changed direction. Long bands of cloud began to shift and obscure the moon. The darkness grew thick and formidable; Mynheer Tripp's eyes were no longer visible—but I felt their continuing reproach. Krebs was quite silent, and every now and again I thought he'd died and had to stop rowing to put my head to his chest and be greeted with, "Still here . . . Don't you worry . . . keep it up, boy—" So back I'd go to my task, abysmally cold and frightened, but not wanting to give the odious Mynheer Tripp the opportunity for gloating.

Then I thought we were saved! Lanterns glinted high up in the night ahead. Our ships at last! I shouted and waved the dim remains of our lantern. Krebs struggled up on his elbow. He said, "It's the Englishman again!"

"Douse the light, Vaarlem!" shrieked Mynheer Tripp. But it was too late. We'd been seen. The Englishman hailed us.

"Ahoy, there!" which in Dutch means, "Stand fast or we'll pepper you with musketfire!"

Nearer and nearer she came, a glinting, ghostly monster. Mynheer Tripp began to gabble we'd be tortured and hanged. I never felt more ashamed of him in my life. He was quaking with terror. I sweated to think of how the English would sneer . . . a craven Dutchman. Maybe I could swear he was French: or German? The great ship was alongside. The murderous cannon still poked out of their ports like blunt black teeth against the dark sky. Two English sailors came down on ropes and hoisted Krebs between them. I was surprised by how like Dutchmen they looked. We were bidden to follow, when Mynheer Tripp further disgraced our nation by being frightened of falling off the rope.

"For God's sake, sir!" I hissed at him. "Make a good showing."

"What d'you mean, 'for God's sake,' Vaarlem?" he hissed back. "You nasty little prig!"

With much contemptuous laughter, more sailors came and helped Mynheer Tripp up between them. I followed on my own. No sooner was I on deck than Mynheer Tripp —who'd got a considerable, jeering crowd about him— shouted in his bad English, "Cover him up! Boy of good family, that! He'll die of cold!" I flushed angrily, but a huge cloth was brought and wrapped round me. To my indignation, I saw it was an English flag. I stripped it off and flung it down.

"I'd rather die of cold than be covered with *that*!" I meant to display *some* Dutch spirit and show we weren't all like Mynheer Tripp.

"Brave lad!" said an officer—the Captain, I think. "Worthier than his companion, eh? What say we heave the old fellow back?"

I grew alarmed. Begged them to do no such thing. "Though you may not think it, he's a great man . . . greater than all of us put together!"

"A greater coward, you mean, boy! How come you go about with such a ragbag?"

But fortunately, Mynheer Tripp hadn't heard the threat. He was by the mizzenmast lantern, examining his drawings to see they were intact. A number of officers and sailors were staring over his shoulder. Then more and more came, with more lanterns, lighting up that patch of deck which seemed roofed with canvas and walled by the netted shrouds. Krebs and his honorable wound and myself and my defiance were left and forgotten. A greater victory was in the making. Of a sudden, I began to feel very proud to be Mynheer Tripp's pupil, and my eyes kept filling with tears on that account. I picked up the flag and wrapped out the cold with it, and went to join the English crowd about my master. Krebs, feeling stronger, leaned on me and stared.

Not all the ships and cannon and defiance in the world could have done what he'd done. With a few lines—no more—he'd advanced into the enemies' hearts and set up his flag there. Mynheer Tripp's victory had been with God's gift—not with the gunsmith's. It's a mercy, I suppose, he never really knew his own power—else he'd have suffocated it under guilders. The Englishmen stared at the drawings, then, seeing Krebs, began comparing with him —in slow English and bad Dutch—the terror and grandeur of their experience, so uncannily caught by the sniffing and shuffling Mynheer Tripp. Pennants, flags, even countries were forgotten. An aspect of battle was seen with neither Dutch nor English eyes, but with a passion and a pity that encompassed all.

"Mynheer Tripp," said the English Captain—a handsome, well-bred man, most likely of Dutch descent, "you are a very great man. We are honored. As our guest, sir, I invite you to visit England."

My master looked at me—not with pride or any so respectable a thing, but with his usual greed and cunning. He said, in his horrible English, "Good! Good! I will paint your Admiral, maybe—?"

And then to me in Dutch, with an offensive smirk, "You see, Vaarlem, these English are different. I told you so. I'll be appreciated—not prosecuted. Just wait till they see what I make of *their* Admiral! Money back, indeed! And after all, my boy, guineas is as good as guilders, eh? Heh-heh!"

He really is the most contemptible man I know! I wonder what the English will make of him—and what he'll make of the English?

The Simpleton

· 1 ·

In the year 1749, on January 18 at Lewes Assizes, my old friend Nicholas Kemp collected seven years' transportation and a sermon from the Judge as long as a monkey's arm.

Poor Nick! He stood there in the dock, his happy young face all bewildered when the jury brought in their verdict, and the Judge said better men had been hanged for less.

Every advantage, the Judge declared he'd had; meaning his family being in a good way of trade (if you care for such things), and as respectable as a church pew.

"But in spite of everything, you've turned out a bad lot, Master Kemp."

Here, Nick looked honestly depressed and surprised that anyone should think so ill of him. Which was a trifle impudent, we thought. After all, he'd only been fourteen when he'd left his home under a cloud—and I don't mean the sort that makes up weather!

He'd prigged some trinkets from his father's workshop (his father being a silversmith), and given them to some flighty doxy of twelve or thereabouts. Yes indeed, if Nick had one weakness above all others, it was for a pretty face. It wasn't a weakness like yours or mine which stays with a wink and a laugh and a kiss and a cuddle; it was a real sighing bog of a weakness. Believe me or not, he was one of your moon-faced lovers who twang and twiddle outside of ladies' windows till someone empties a chamber pot on them to keep them quiet.

On this, his first mistake, he'd been unlucky enough to pick on the daughter of the trinkets' lawful owner—who took offense and worse. He left that very night, with his heart, I'm sure, carved on a dozen trees.

"If I didn't think there was some goodness in your

soul," went on the Judge, "I'd have you hanged out of hand."

Well, well—he was a judge and had had his bellyful of human nature. If he saw goodness in Nick's soul, it must have been there.

"So it's seven years in Virginia for you, Nicholas Kemp," finished up the Judge. "And may you be improved by it."

Nick gave a great sigh and looked as glum and heart-broken as if the hangman had asked for his neck.

"Poor soul!" muttered someone at the back. "I'd have sworn he was innocent."

Which was exactly what Nick *had* sworn—till he'd been peached on by the rosy-cheeked trollop he'd birth-day'd with a silver watch he'd prigged the previous morning. We'd warned him she was a low-class slut, but not being exactly a gentleman himself, he'd no yardstick to judge her by. Even got peeved and told us to be content with the guineas he'd passed on and leave the watch to him. She was one of Nature's ladies, he said, and had promised not to wear the watch for a fortnight.

It was a large watch, as I remember it; a shade vulgar, like Nick. She wore it as soon as his back was turned—and in the parlor of the "White Horse," which was where it had been prigged. Need I say more?

A peace officer with a neck like a bull came to our lodgings. Nick shot under the table.

'Ad we any notion of a young 'un called Kemp? If so, it were our dooty to give 'im up.

I ask you—what could we do? Nick looked a trifle put out, at first, but then took it in good part when we reminded him we'd told him so. I fancy he knew where the blame really lay. Lord! you should have seen the look he hung on that trollop when she gave her evidence! Stones would have wept. (Though, I must admit, we couldn't resist a chuckle.) But jurors' hearts are made of sterner stuff . . .

So we took a coach down to Deal to see him off. The *Phoenix* out of Deptford was anchored there, dipping and bobbing like an enormous bridesmaid, all laced and gilded and wanting only her fat bodice and petticoat to be put on that she might billow out to some roaring wedding at sea.

But she wasn't the doxy after Nick's heart, and his face was as long as a coffin when he shuffled, leg-ironed, into the rowboat with half a dozen assorted embezzlers, pickpockets, and ragged layabouts, all Virginia bound.

We waved, but I don't think he saw us, so we left it till next morning when we hired a fisherman to row us out to the *Phoenix* to send our poor friend off in convivial style.

A tremendous great brute of a ship was the *Phoenix*—when we got close—and as far past her prime as was reasonable with still being afloat. She creaked and grunted and groaned even in the calm waters, so what she would do when the wind blew, God and her Captain alone knew.

But there was no sense or kindness in frightening poor Nick, so we all toasted him in gin and drank to the teeming doxies in Virginia—far fairer than our English drabs—and kept to ourselves the belief he'd not make halfway over with his soul and body in one piece.

I don't know whether he was still in irons then, for we could only see his head and shoulders poking out of a gun port, six feet aloft.

"Cheer up, Nick!" one of us shouted. "There's a Richmond in Virginia with a lass that's peach to porridge to the blowsy damsel here!"

But he looked like his silly heart would break.

"Cheer up, Nick!" I roared. "Gentlemen pay fifty pounds for a trip like yours!"

I think he was going to smile. He'd a fair sense of humor, which was part of the reason we kept his acquaintance—that and his skill in keeping us in funds—yes, I'm sure he was going to smile, when another convict poked his head out beside him and spat mightily into the sea; so we all had to duck to avoid.

"Friends of your'n, sonny?" asked this fellow curiously, but poor Nick never answered a word. His heart was too full, we guessed.

So, "Cheer up, Nick!" shouted the last of us. "You're dead lucky, you know! After all, as the good Judge said, you might have been nubbed, old dear! For you wasn't exactly innocent, was you, Nick? Ha-ha!"

It was then that he spoke.

"Aye," he said, in that rich voice of his that was always so surprising. "I wasn't innocent, was I? Not like you, friends."

"What d'you mean, Nick?"

"Just what I say, *friends*."

The privation in that stinking hold was having its effect on him, all right . . . It's always said that, put a mouse with rats and it grows sharper teeth and a longer tail. He leaned on *friends* very verminously indeed. We were all sorry to note it.

"You could have saved me, friends. You needn't have given me up."

"Come along, Nick! Would you have us be accessories? We'd have been took along with you! And what would our families have said to that? Besides, I'm sure your feet was poking out of the table. And anyways, it was on ac-

count of the watch. Remember? We warned you. It was
the watch that did it. And we'd no part in that, my lad!"

"No," said Nick, somewhat sourly for him. "Your
hands were clean. For once."

A nasty dig, that. But we all made allowances, I think.
We didn't want to show bitterness to a friend in distress.
So we smiled and toasted him again and gave the boatman
the nod to pull away. No sense in drawing out what had
turned so sour . . .

Then, as we began to shift off, he shouted after us, "I
may be a scapegoat, friends—but there's some sins I'll not
carry off for you! There's some sins that'll always come
home to roost!"

Here was an unchristian sentiment if ever there was
one! In what Scripture, for God's sake, does the scapegoat
turn round and snarl? Something devilish there.

Nonetheless, we kept our charity and drank Nick's
salvation deep into the night, remembering good times
together and ending up quite merry. I speak no less than
the truth when I say we all had a warm corner in our
hearts for that simpleton, Nicholas Kemp. We forgave
his turning on us and put it down to the ugly circumstance
of his confinement, rather than to a nature grown unsteady.

Next morning, which was the twenty-first and a Thurs-
day, we rose at ten and went down to the frontage of the

sea, warmly meaning to row out once more and let by-gones be bygones and give poor Nick a second chance to carry a gentle thought of us all into the hereafter.

But alas! it was not to be. The *Phoenix* had already spread her grubby finery and lumbered out to sea. When she was pointed out to us, she was no bigger than a thumb-nail. We waved—and I recall our eyes grew moist with staring.

"The last of Nick Kemp," sighed one of us. "Let's go drink to his memory. Let's not forget he served us well, and in his simple way was faithful. But now he's gone, and I fancy the world's seen the end of him. Poor old Nick!"

"We'll not forget you, Nick," I said, in sentimental mood. "Never let it be said that your lack of breeding spoiled the goodness of your heart."

"Farewell, Nick Kemp," murmured the last of us, solemnly. "Though the sea will most likely gobble up you and the dingy *Phoenix* in a day, I fancy, you'll live on in our hearts. For it'll be a long while before we find another such dear simple soul to take your place. So come, lads! Let's start looking!"

· 2 ·

Contrary to the confident expectations of the kind friends who'd seen him off, a day had passed and Nicholas Kemp was still alive and the *Phoenix* still afloat—though when the wind blew and the sea heaved, the groaning of the ship and the convicts together was such as to make any man think the end of the world was nigh.

Eighty-two of them slept, rolled, moaned, stank, and swore between the main- and foremasts, on what had once been the lower gun deck. But the 32-pounders were gone, and out of the gun ports now, instead of ball and grape-shot, flew ancient hats, shrieks, old boots, bellows of song, bottles with painful messages, rats, pewter plates, and stinking pots to litter the old sea in a long, dancing line.

They were a vilely quarrelsome lot, were the convicts, having come from four stone prisons into this wooden one. And each of these prisons, which were Newgate, Marshalsea, the Fleet, and Lewes, had printed a fierce and rank comradeship on its own platoon. Thus the Newgate gentry jeered at the Marshalsea, who spat on the Fleet, who, in their turn, did what they could to make life wretcheder than it need have been for the six from Lewes Jail.

Yet this last sturdy little band stood up remarkably well and gave as good as it took, or rather, took somewhat more than was taken from it—thieving being as common as breathing and Sussex thieves being the busiest of all . . .

Nonetheless, small as it was, even this band carried its passenger; one who was among them, so to speak, but not of them. One whose heart had fallen farther than his boots and was languishing over a large part of southern England, carved into trees, scratched onto doors, marked up in ale on tavern windows, and once, painted in blood (thinly—from a scratch) on an alderman's coach. Nicholas Kemp crouched lost in his tender past. While round about him the profoundest activities went on, he mooned away in his private night, where the stars were bright, bright eyes.

Yet there must have been something about him that touched even the hardest heart. No one kicked him; no one trod on him; no one clouted him round the head. Instead, to his great surprise, he found himself in the midst of a kind of plenty. Tattered blankets and stolen dinners were passed stealthily on with a "Take it, son. It's going begging."

These gifts from a darker heaven, so to speak, began to fall soon after the ramshackle commotion on deck declared the *Phoenix* to be under way and the wind set fair for Virginia.

First a neckerchief and then a pair of mittens were dropped in his lap.

"Put 'em on, sonny, afore you catch your death of cold."

Later came a smelly waistcoat.

"Roll it up, sonny. 'Twill serve as a pillow."

Most gratefully (gratitude being another of his weaknesses) Nick looked up, and a pair of beady eyes looked briefly—almost contemptuously down. Nicholas Kemp, amiable soul that he was, seemed to have brought out the father in a squat fierce embezzler called Bartleman.

He was much moved by this strange circumstance, and it served to calm his confused and agitated thoughts concerning the three kind friends whose miserable cowardice and stinking treachery had put him where he was.

He confided as much to Bartleman during the first pitchy night out of Deal, and felt easier in his mind for it.

"How'd you like to slit their throats, son?" came the embezzler's harsh voice. Then, before Nicholas could reply one way or the other, came a laugh that had a very fatal ring to it.

But, disquieting as was this laugh, the next day brought a blanket and a pipe and enough "son's" and "sonny's" to furnish a madman's sky.

On this second day, which turned out to be brisk and

blowy and laid half the convicts low, Bartleman's example inspired another of the Lewes company to pass on to Nicholas a quarter bottle of gin. Bartleman was formidably angry. He snatched up the bottle and bade the giver leave the lad to him. On which Nicholas felt uneasily that Bartleman had bought him, lock, stock, and barrel, as a receptacle for his own charity.

Later that day came an incident even more striking. It had to do with the pipe. Though not much of a smoker (he preferred snuff when he could get it), Nicholas found there was some comfort to be had from sucking at the pipe while he squatted and contemplated the rusting iron of his fetters. The flavor of the tobacco brought back memories of inns and taverns. The memory of a tavern brought back the memory of a pair of cherry lips and hair like a fold of the night. His last heartbreak, and though she'd helped to betray him he forgave her with a sigh . . .

"Bleeding thief," came a voice thick with reproach. He looked up. Before him stood a bony, hideous ruffian from the Marshalsea company. He'd shuffled up unheard; there was such a grinding and clinking and clanking of leg irons that all motions turned out stealthy—their sounds being swallowed up in the general uproar.

"Thief?" said Nicholas, reddening awkwardly. His accuser's fists were large, and roughened from easy use.

"You got my pipe, ain't you? You prigged it yesterday and left me in a very pitiable state, mister. I been through a horrible night on your account. I twitched and groaned and me poor mouth felt like old leather. And now I sees you, rosy as the bleeding dawn and a-smoking of my pipe like it was your very own. You done wrong, mister, and I'm a-going to beat you into a pulp for it."

"I—I found it," attempted Nicholas, never having been remarkable for his quickness in inventing excuses. He smiled hopefully, then feebly, then not at all as he saw he'd had no luck.

So he began to shrink backward, praying that he was somehow in the grip of a nightmare from which he'd shortly awaken and find himself a thousand miles away.

But no such awakening came. The nightmare went on apace. Though well made and tolerably sturdy, he lacked a fierce nature. Violence dismayed him. The Marshalsea ruffian frightened the wits out of him.

Abruptly, he found himself hard against a bulkhead. He must have traveled six yards on his shaking bottom, with the monster coming on. Fifteen or twenty bleary faces regarded him with interest. None with compassion.

"Oh God," whispered Nicholas, thinking he ought to be putting his affairs in order, for the Marshalsea man had hold of a short length of timber, studded with nails.

"God help me . . . God help me . . ." he went on, being no richer in prayer than he was in excuses. "God help—"

"The lad said he found it, friend."

Irritably, the Marshalsea man turned aside. Bartleman was there. Bartleman was grinning. Horrible sight. He'd sharp, ratlike teeth.

"The lad said he found it, friend," repeated Bartleman. "And if you don't take his word, I'll cut your throat out. So help me, I will." Bartleman continued to grin. He had a knife, and it was plain he'd be happy to use it.

Much surprised, the Marshalsea man peered at Bartleman, and then at his onetime supporters. They looked absorbed—as if they'd never seen a throat cut before.

He licked his lips with a venomous rapidity and began to shuffle sideways, seeking to make a circle about the squat embezzler. But his leg irons dragged on him, giving his motions the air of a tipsy country dance.

Amiably, Bartleman watched him, even seemed sympathetic.

"Them bracelets is cruel when you're oversize, friend. Which you should have thought on afore you came accusing sonny here."

"I got no quarrel with you, mister," said the Marshalsea man, not pausing in his circling.

Nicholas stared at his champion with gloomy uncertainty. Bartleman was the smaller. Bartleman hadn't the reach. And Bartleman had been asked, most politely, to mind his own business. If he, Nicholas Kemp, had been Bartleman, he'd have been well content to sheer off and leave the Marshalsea monster to his lawful prey—N. Kemp.

But Bartleman owned a different soul, and altogether outside of Nicholas's dreaming. He continued to watch the Marshalsea man round and round, while the convicts pushed and clanked for a better view.

The Marshalsea man's eyes were glittering sharply. Of a sudden, Nicholas divined there was fear in them. He felt weirdly sorry for him—even though he himself was the alarmed object of the man's rage. He understood his plight. Unluckily, he must have set himself up among his own company as something of a leader, a hero even, a man of iron, a man not to be trifled with. He could not afford to be as discreet with Bartleman as, maybe, he'd have liked. He must needs be formidable. He had no choice, now.

"I said I got no quarrel with you, mister," he repeated fiercely. "My quarrel's with that thieving runt yonder."

There being no mistaking who was meant, Nicholas groaned and made to stand up—not, as the saying goes, meaning to sell his life dearly, but wondering how best he might haggle to keep it. After all, he'd not stolen the pipe—Bartleman had prigged it. Bartleman had—

"Sit you down, son. No call to stand when I'm standing for you."

Bartleman's wide back was toward him. His coat had a dim shine. The seam had done good service, but was plainly ready for retirement. Over his shoulder, peering for Nicholas, stretched the shaggy, uneasy head of the Marshalsea man.

Then, of a disagreeable sudden, Bartleman seemed to weary of defending the wretched Nicholas. He bowed aside with, "Here, son, gentleman wants a word with you. I should be quick about it if I was you!"

Whether the Marshalsea man came on at once, or whether he was helped by Bartleman, was hard to say. There was too much of deftness and speed in the embezzler's movements to be sure. The Marshalsea man lumbered past him with a distressful grunt.

Such was his strength and determination that he got as far as Nicholas and even managed to seize hold of the offending pipe before the neat hole in his side let out the last of his life's blood. Bartleman had done him in as he'd passed.

"I told you to be quick about it," said Bartleman, wip-

ing his knife on his sleeve. "Now you'll never hear that word he wanted."

But Nicholas had already heard it, breathed out on the man's escaping soul.

"You stinking little fool—" he'd sighed . . .

This formidable incident, which, while it lasted, seemed to cast a queer glare of its own, ended rapidly and in furtive, grunting shadows.

Bartleman, who was possessed of unusual strength, lifted the ragged dead man (whose name had been Dorman or Gorman—no one knew for certain) and bundled him up to a gun port.

Two men hastened to assist—but there was no need. The Marshalsea man was gone horribly quick, and the splash of him followed briefly on—a yard, maybe, aft of the portage that had served for a graveside.

No word of this abrupt and fearful diminishing reached the upper deck. What with the continual flying out of all manner of rubbish, and the intolerable confusion in the convicts' hold, the loss of a soul could not possibly have been known save by peachment. And there was no man there who'd peach on Bartleman.

There was something shrewdly devilish about the embezzler, something quick and to the point that made the notion of informing on him a dream to turn a man's blood to ice.

But there was also admiration. Transportable crimes being, by and large, piddling matters of vagrancy, sneak thieving, perjury, and the like, murder flew up like a scarlet banner, and Bartleman stood suddenly forth as a prince of felons, a captain in the army of sin.

This admiration showed itself chiefly in a general eagerness to refer private quarrels to the embezzler for his just decision. He'd shown himself a man quick to take up arms for the oppressed and the weak, and it was wonderful how many discovered themselves to be weak and oppressed when there was a champion in sight.

It was generally agreed that the dead man had asked for what he got and no blame could be attached to his obliger. The cause had been virtuous, and the execution without malice and commendably prompt.

Nicholas Kemp regarded his strange protector with the most remarkable mixture of feelings ever stirred into a mortal soul. The chief of these was terror, with a seasoning of awe, some pride, a pinch of conceit at having been chosen, a dash of honest bewilderment as to why, and small but strong, a twist of guilt that a man had died on his account.

This last he could not rid himself of, and the taste of it

—together with the Marshalsea man's last words which had been more pitying than bitter—lingered long. Then, little by little, his thoughts were changed back into dreams, and his dreams were as ever the old wistful memories of the sweet but far-off ladies to each of whom he'd given his heart. Truly, never was the nature of a transported felon as blindly gentle as Nicholas Kemp's.

On the fourth day out—the convicts seeming quiet and genteel—the Captain ordered all leg irons to be removed and stored in a compartment directly aft. He was well pleased to afford this touch of humanity, and considered himself blessed with a peaceable cargo. Most marvelously, the vilely quarrelsome parties in the dark of the lower gun deck were subdued. He put it down to the motion of the sea, which, to him, was as gentle as the rocking of a crib.

He did not know that, from many snapping beasts, the convicts had been compounded into one, a corporate monster with a host of hands and a single heart.

Bartleman the embezzler of money had advanced himself. He had become an embezzler of souls.

· 3 ·

The Captain of the *Phoenix* was a merciful man. On Wednesday, January 27, in the morning, the convicts from the lower gun deck were suffered to come up on a portion of the main deck, between the forecastle and a roped barrier midway to the mainmast. For three days now, they had been out of irons and as quiet and decent as mice. There was no reason to suppose they'd take more advantage of the open air than God had intended; namely, to breathe it peaceably and keep in health.

Nonetheless, the Captain confided his humane intention to his paying passengers the night before and promised stern precautions against the molesting of young females—of whom three were amiable and one was charming, a Miss Caroline Warboys.

"Even so," he went on, glancing sharpishly to Miss Warboys, "I would be obliged if you would maintain a discreet distance from the barrier. Please to remember there are many pickpockets among my convicts; some are most likely diseased—and all of 'em whiff like nine o'clock! So I begs of you, gentlemen and chiefly you soft ladies, don't let your milky kindness get the better of your good sense."

Here, he looked particularly hard at Miss Warboys, who glanced down as if innocent that her pert prettiness had turned the heads of the ship's crew so far about that they scarce knew larboard from starboard. So plentiful was her sweet kindness that she could not forebear from flashing her smiles at any gentleman in range of them. (It was said that on a clear day her smile could rake the ship from stem to stern.)

The morning proved handsome though cold. A brisk breeze blew across the deck, swelling out the mainsail in its larboard cheek like a giant's toothache. But the sea was easy and the *Phoenix* scissored away, turning the waters back from her bows in high silver folds, while behind her busy stern made lace of it . . .

At ten o'clock, the Captain glanced approvingly to the shrouds, where six of his sailors were fixed with muskets leveled down on the space the convicts were to occupy. Miss Warboys also looked up and smiled—thereby causing one of the sailors to slip and nearly hang himself in an effort to strike a more remarkable attitude.

"Open up the hatch!" called the Captain.

"Open up that bleeding hatch!" repeated the boatswain.

"Open it up and let them poor stinking felons out!" Then —"Godalmighty what a noseful!"

This last as the hatch was slid back and the air grew hazy with the rising heat.

One by one, the convicts came up. They were dark and filthy. They shrank from the wind. Sought to hide their heads in their scanty coats till they looked like a congregation of hunchbacks. They scowled blackly against the sunlight—which was harsh and strange to them.

One by one they continued to come, till the space allotted was almost filled. At last, no more of them came. The boatswain had counted eight-one. He shrugged his shoulders. Two and eighty there should have been, but he was not confident enough in his arithmetic to remark on it. Two must have come up together, he decided . . . and went about his business, leaving the gaping passengers to be fascinated, shocked, and entertained by the sight of the felons taking the air.

Little by little, as they grew accustomed to the light, the convicts' frowns diminished, and as the wind's edge blunted to them they began to hold up their heads like a field of shaggy blossoms, much blasted by foul weather yet hopeful of the sun.

The passengers, who had shrunk back at the first emerging, now plucked up their courage and plucked out their pocket handkerchiefs (which they held to their noses) and moved nearer the barrier. And the convicts jostled and grinned and tossed them strong pleasantries for the joy of making the ladies blush.

One man in particular was doing remarkably well at this sport, scarleting cheeks like a field of poppies with language as ripe as old fish . . .

"Enough of that!" snapped a squat, square-faced convict who seemed to escape jostling more easily than most. He'd moved forward and now, with broad, powerful hands, pushed two surprised female passengers farther off the rope—as if for their own benefit.

The foul-mouthed one looked sharply round—then stopped like he'd been cut off with a knife.

"Sorry, Mister Bartleman, sir. 'Twas only a game . . . sorry, sir—"

Miss Warboys flashed one of her pertest smiles at this squat convict who seemed to be exceptional. But either he missed it entirely, or he was cased in stouter armor than ever she'd come upon before. Rather, the sailors in the shrouds, the Captain on the quarter-deck, and the general furnishing of the ship itself seemed to take him more than Miss Warboys's brightest smile.

But it had not been altogether wasted. Someone else had been hit. A friend, follower, or acquaintance of this squat convict. A young—pitifully young—man with a week-old beard that fringed his pleasant face like goose-berry fluff.

He caught her eye, paled, seemed to tremble—then went most gratifyingly red. He smiled hopefully—and she, being kind, smiled back.

Had there been not so close a press, she'd have been further pleased to see his knees shaking with excitement.

Unlikely as was the time and the place, Nicholas Kemp's chief weakness had found him out once more. A pretty face had so bewitched him that, had the sun been a pendant, he'd have stole it for Miss Warboys and let the world go hang in the dark.

Being female (and Miss Warboys was as female a lass as ever tipped a hoop), she was the lass for him. Even the terrible Bartleman straightway took a second place in his thoughts—and all things seemed temporary till he should see her more.

During that evening and night, his situation among the convicts—which on account of Bartleman's friendship stood high—helped him make some improvements to his appearance. He obtained the interest of a onetime barber who'd kept some tools of his trade.

Bartleman looked on indulgently while Nicholas's hair was being trimmed and his face scraped over.

"I take it it's for the doxy with the roving eye," he said with a contemptuous good humor.

Nicholas nodded. ("Nearly lorst an ear, mister," muttered the barber, twitching with fright.)

"She's a sharp pennyworth, sonny. Too sharp for you."

"What d'you mean?" asked Nicholas, peevish and offended on Miss Warboys's behalf. Though he feared Bartleman to the bottom of his soul, his chief weakness gave him a certain strength; which strength even his three kind friends had sometime remarked on. To the barber's surprise, the meek Master Kemp had the foolhardiness to frown at the murderous embezzler.

But more surprising still, Bartleman only grinned and ruffled Nick's hair almost apologetically.

"No offense, sonny. No call for fury. Save it for the red-haired doxy. 'Twill impress her no end. But then what?" He chuckled. "Shall you offer her your heart? Hm! She's made of shrewder stuff than that! I'm afraid you'll have to do better. Tell you what—offer her this alongside of your heart . . . and then maybe you've got a chance! Here—take it, son! It's going begging!"

The extraordinary Bartleman was holding out a brooch —a charming golden key, set with garnet and pearl.

"Not worth a king's ransom, maybe—but doxies come a bit cheaper, you know. Take it, I say!"

Helplessly, Nicholas reached up—for there was suddenly a glitter of anger in Bartleman's eyes, as if the brooch meant more to him than he was willing to say, and under no circumstances would he endure a refusal of it. Nicholas took the brooch—and pricked himself lightly on its pin. Vaguely, he felt he'd taken a deposit on his soul.

The next day proved wild and blowy and not at all prosperous for courting. The convicts only staggered up on deck to be ridded of the formidable clanking of their leg irons which strained at their securings behind the bulkhead. A loud and fearful sound that seemed to beat inside their very heads.

Of passengers, only the hardiest were visible. Miss Warboys was not among them. But her absence served only to increase Nicholas's fondness and diminish his doubts concerning the brooch. He was now in the second stage of love at first sight, which commonly took the form, with him, of advertising his heart on walls, trees, and doors. Which aching part of him he engraved on the deckboards, with the pin of Bartleman's brooch.

So it was on the Friday, then, with the weather fair and the sea taking a high polish from the sun, that Nicholas Kemp caught Miss Warboys's eye for a second time.

Still in genial mood, Bartleman had eased his young friend's passage to the rope. Here, Nicholas stood for close on twenty minutes while the passengers came out of the poop to consider the morning. Then he was rewarded.

Last of all, and demure as was possible in scarlet cloak and yellow windbonnet, came Miss Warboys, tipping neatly down the companionway with a glint of silken ankles and a general air of curtseying to the world for its attention.

"Trollop!" remarked one of the female passengers, but Miss Warboys did not choose to hear.

Instead, she glanced up to the shrouds, where the watchful sailors hung, to the poop where the Captain walked with his officers, to the great foresail upon which the vague shadow of the main topsail lay like the ghost of a first intention, to the sky—to the sea—to their hazy joining; in short, she looked everywhere but to the desperately young convict whose eyes ate up the distance between him and her.

And *then* her eye lighted on him—and lighted *in* him such a fire that its glow reached clean across the chilly deck till her cheeks rosied over like wine on a napkin . . .

"And well might she blush!" remarked another female passenger. "The brassy minx!"

But, though scarce fifteen yards separated Miss Warboys from Nicholas Kemp, so disparate were their situations that it might have been fifteen miles . . . or five hundred, even . . .

In vain, the young man stared—with eyes grown huge with longing. Miss Warboys could but smile (albeit wistfully, for the young convict moved her more than she'd bargained for) and gently shake her head. There could be no commerce between a lady and a convict save by looking.

But there was no dousing the light in the young man's face. Nicholas Kemp had gone directly into his third stage of love at first sight, which was pretty nearly mortal. It was the stage in which he'd have plunged into the sea for her, gone through fire for her, fought off venomous monsters for her—had she but raised her little finger.

Somewhat sadly, Miss Warboys looked down. There was a distant gleam in her eyes, as if, had the young man not been a convict, her little finger would have gone up like a flagpole. Again, she shook her head. The lady and the convict were never meant to meet.

There must be a place where Heaven abuts onto Hell, where angels and the damned may look deep into one another's eyes and say, "There, but for the grace of God, might be I." Miss Warboys bit her lip, then raised her hand to hide it. If only the young man would bid her good morning in a genteel fashion—or even bow, then they might become acquainted. If only he would stop staring at her so mournfully with eyes that declared—for all the world to see—"I love you and will love you till I die." If only—

If only, thought Nicholas, she would nod or bid me good morning. If only something remarkable would happen. If only—

In his tender extremity, he'd wafted out his hand as if to summon up a miracle from somewhere. It was the hand in which he'd been holding his pipe. Unluckily, it caught against the rope. The pipe dropped and fell maybe a yard beyond the rope. It was out of his reach. A kindly passenger made to help . . . but was forestalled.

A swift rustling passed him by, and a smell of roses was briefly on the air.

"That forward hussy!" remarked a third female passenger. "*She* didn't need much invitation!"

But Miss Warboys never heard her. Having picked up the young convict's pipe, she'd given it to him—and with it, her hand, which he held with some determination.

"My name is Nicholas Kemp—Nicholas Kemp," he said very rapidly—as if he'd brought the good news a great distance and was anxious to deliver it. "From Preston in Sussex. Nicholas Kemp—"

"Caroline Warboys," said she, with the chief weight on Caroline.

(Though she spoke soft, "Caroline" was taken up by several convicts and tried out humorously.)

"Caroline—"

"—Yes, Mister Kemp?"

"No—no! I was going to say it's a sweet name. And suits you well, Miss Warboys."

"It was on account of the Queen, you know. I was called after the Queen—"

"—Queens should be called after you!"

"Neatly spoke, sonny!"

Bartleman had passed by. He'd grinned, as if well pleased with himself. His passage had been brief—but of consequence.

Till he'd come, Nicholas and Miss Warboys had stood, it seemed to them, in some springtime field, or by a gentle river quite overhung with willow in which unusually musical birds were singing—or anywhere, in short, save the worldly ship with its windy stench and peevish jostlings.

Miss Warboys withdrew her hand from Nicholas's.

"Will you be—er—long in—in Virginia, Mister Kemp?"

"Seven years."

"Was you very wicked, Mister Kemp?"

Bitterly, he shook his head. The spell had been broken. Gone was the mysterious springtime. He frowned. Miss Warboys did likewise. The wind had somehow got inside of her bonnet. Her cheeks felt chilled. A sharp melancholy invaded her . . . though the exact nature of it was outside of her telling. Now she wondered what she was doing, standing so close to the convicts' rope, even with tears in her eyes.

"I hope your pipe wasn't broke, Mister Kemp."

He said it wasn't.

"If you'll pardon me now, Mister Kemp—I must go back—"

"—Will I not see you again?"

"I expect so, Mister Kemp. The ship's a small world. Good morning to you—"

"—Miss Warboys!"

"Yes, Mister Kemp?"

"Miss Warboys—Please—I beg of you—If you'd do me the honor . . . I'd be happy—so happy—and—and there's no one else, I assure you! Please, *please* accept this!"

In a last desperation to recapture what he dreaded had been lost, he was holding out Bartleman's brooch!

"It was my—my mother's!" he added hopefully.

Miss Warboys looked at it. Saw it was charming. She looked up at Nicholas. Found him even more so. She struggled with herself. She hesitated . . .

In all justice, vanity had something to do with her decision. In all honesty, greed had something to do with it. But in all truth, affection and even the beginnings of love gave the final push.

"I really shouldn't, Mister Kemp . . . I really oughtn't —But—but as you've no one else . . . and—and it *was* your mother's, and—and—there, but for the grace of God might be any gentleman—Indeed, Mister Kemp, the honor's quite mine, you know!"

She took the brooch and, as she did so, Nicholas briefly kissed her hand.

So what was Bartleman now? A fallen angel—or a rising devil? The bloodstained pipe and the brooch. Both had been the embezzler's gift. Both had helped to bring him Miss Warboys.

Absently, he put the pipe in his mouth. His teeth encountered the deep dents made by the Marshalsea man's before him. For a moment, he fancied alien thoughts to be blowing through his mind—thoughts of some fierceness, such as a stabbed man might have had if he could . . . ("You stinking little fool—")

Hurriedly, Nicholas put the pipe away, and with it much of his disquiet. Very soon he reasoned himself out of uneasiness over Bartleman, and reflected that the embezzler had been good to him. To distrust him was ungrateful. Bartleman had put a sun in his gray sky. And what a sun!

He turned his thoughts—without much hardship—to Miss Warboys, and in happy frame of mind composed himself for sleep. It was close on midnight, and the convict hold most quiet. Nicholas sighed, then sighed again, and slipped away into his mysterious springtime . . .

This was a great gift of his—to push uneasiness under a cushion of hope; even to sleep when other men might well have stayed awake . . .

· 4 ·

He was visited by the sweetest of dreams. He rode a white horse out of darkling woods across wide, spangled fields. And as he jogged along, his horse's harness jingled cheerfully (which may or may not have been the clinking of the leg irons in the compartment aft). Then he was in a trim, fair garden where sunshine and the cypresses played chess across the lawn; and a fountain splashed most musically (which may or may not have been the dark ocean slapping the vessel's sides).

Now he was in an avenue of scarlet and yellow rose trees, walking with Miss Warboys and talking with Miss Warboys, and offering Miss Warboys the keys of his heart. And she, with a rustle of silk and a twinkling of eyes, was declaring, "I really shouldn't . . . I really oughtn't . . . but seeing as how—"

Then a shadow fell across their path as from between

the trees stepped a squat lackey, looking remarkably like Bartleman, with another key.

"Here, son. Give her this. It's the key of Heaven. Take it. It's going begging!"

"Thank 'ee, my man," said Nick, in his dream. "Much obliged. Miss Warboys, pray accept this further trifle!"

Miss Warboys's eyes shone with pleasure that was enchanting to behold. The key was charming, set with garnet and pearl.

"Just sign this receipt, sonny. Evidence that I gave it, y'know—"

The lackey held out a pen and paper that he'd produced from nowhere.

"Sign!"

"But there's nothing on the paper—"

"You ain't signed it, yet."

"But where's the ink, my man?"

"Ink, sonny? You sign for this in blood!"

With that, he promptly stuck the pen into Nicholas's finger.

"Sign, son—"

"—That hurt! I'm bleeding! Stop it—stop it, I say! It hurt—"

"—There's worse to come, N. Kemp. Worse to come! Get up, you lousy thief! On your feet!"

Voices outside of his dream were shouting in his ear. Hands outside of his dream were dragging him to his feet—

"On your feet, Kemp! Move, or by God, you'll suffer!"

"That hurt! Stop, I say—" cried Nicholas, confusedly, for he was still but half awake and much distracted.

The convicts' hold seemed filled with swinging lanterns and angry faces. Someone had hold of his shoulder with a grip of iron. It was the boatswain.

"The yardarm for you, my lad! You may have 'scaped Tyburn, but the *Phoenix*'ll finish you off! Move, I say!"

He moved. Was dragged up the companionway into the freezing night air. It was but half an hour after midnight.

He remembered being surprised to see the stars and a wedge of the moon shining both aloft and in the sea. A pair of kissing heavens—yet such was his bewilderment, he knew not which was which . . .

He'd not the faintest notion of what was afoot, nor of the peril in which he stood.

"So you are Nicholas Kemp," said the Captain, as if he'd long been trying to find a face to fit that name.

This was on the quarter-deck. The Captain was much muffled and plainly feeling the chill. Though it was of no consequence, Nicholas recalled very clearly the Captain muttering to an officer of his, "No, mister. Cold or no, we'll do it out here. They whiff so strong, y'know, that, take 'em inside and the whole place stinks for a month! Like cats, y'know . . ."

Under the staring moonlight, the *Phoenix* was a silver ship with a silver deck, much hacked and slashed with the black shadows flung by the lofty tentage of masts, sails, and shrouds. In and out of these shadows, phantom-like, came more of the ship's officers to gather in a formidable group about the stout little Captain.

"Call Miss Warboys," he said—somewhat wearily.

At once, into Nicholas's shaking brain came the unlikely hope that the Captain was intending to marry them.

But even his extraordinary optimism and unusual capacity for overlooking plain disaster suffered a setback when Miss Warboys came.

Her face, under its hood, was worried and mournful. Nor was it improved by sight of Nicholas. She scowled and began, quietly, to cry.

"Is this him, Miss Warboys?"

She nodded, and Nicholas's heart began to beat unequally. What had he done?

The Captain turned from the lady to the convict.

"You gave her a brooch?"

"Indeed I did, sir. Oh yes, yes—"

"—This brooch?"

The Captain was holding out the charming trifle that Bartleman had given him.

"That's it, sir! Why—"

But before he could finish asking, the Captain violently told him.

The damnable brooch had been prigged! When, for God's sake? The very first day the convicts had come on deck. A paying passenger had been robbed by the rope. At first, she'd said nothing—on account of being ashamed of ignoring the Captain's advice. But then, in the Great Cabin that very night (not two hours ago), an unpleasant scene. The paying passenger—a lady of means—had spied the brooch, her brooch, on Miss Warboys. Called her a thief. Miss Warboys had gone white as a topsail. Witnesses—the lady's husband (a man of means), her daughter, her friends had all confirmed the brooch's ownership. Miss Warboys had burst into tears. Swore the brooch had been a gift. Who from? Nicholas Kemp. And who was he when he was at home? Here, Miss Warboys had looked ill. Piteously. Swallowed hard so's her pretty neck had jumped. A—a convict—

The Captain ran on awhile longer, with detail on damning detail. But Nicholas no longer heard him plainly. Instead, an old familiar dismay invaded him. Once more, his need to offer more than he owned had been his downfall.

Mournfully, he heard at last, as in a harsher dream than ever he'd had before, the Captain grate, "Take him below. Put him in irons, I'll have him hanged in the morning. So help me, I will!"

"It's no use crying, miss," a grim voice declared as he was dragged away. "He's had his chance in this world. Tomorrow, in the clean fresh air, he'll get his chance for the next. From a rope at the end of that pole up yonder."

"I ain't crying for him," came a tearful reply; then, with bewildered melancholy, "I'm crying for myself, sir."

There was an iron ring bolted to the mainmast where it sank through the compartment aft of the convicts' hold. To this ring was fixed four foot of chain—and to this chain, by his left ankle, was fettered Nicholas Kemp.

For company he had—in this dark place—some half dozen busy rats, the two grinding hillocks of leg irons (which were lashed to boltheads in the vessel's ribs on either side), and his thoughts.

These were of a somber, frantic cast. They were deep inasmuch as they were low; they were far-reaching inasmuch as they reached far back to the first first-sight love to whom he'd given his heart (and more) . . . then on through many such buds and lovely blossoms to the black-haired beauty of Lewes and now Miss Warboys herself . . . A bouquet of sweet disaster.

For a while, he attempted to sing in time to the regular uproar of the lashed irons. But such songs as he knew were all ballads of forsaken love, neglected love, despised love, graveyard love, fruitless love, betrayed love, impossible love, love at death's door—in short, his songs were all of a love that was scarce more prosperous than his own. Did he but know it, he was passed beyond the third stage of first-sight love. He was now in its fourth stage, from which there is no turning back and for which not even death is a sure cure; it lingers on in the air . . .

He paused in his singing and listened once more to the solemn grinding of the invisible irons. Between their clankings, he could hear the industrious rats. They seemed to be at dinner. He shuddered to imagine the course. He sat down and attempted to compose himself for sleep. Then considered he'd no cause to wish the morning nearer. Yet waking held no profit, either . . .

His thoughts kept turning back with dismal anger to the three kind friends who'd seen him off at Deal. Seen him off indeed! He saw them now, as he'd seen them so often before—those three well-born young gentlemen—sitting easy in some coffeehouse, jingling the guineas he'd prigged for them and waiting for more.

"Well done, Nick, old dear!"

"Lord! You're a marvel, Nick!"

"Don't know what we'd do without you, Nick!"

Desolately, he stared into the darkness and wondered who had made the world and why. Where was his mysterious springtime gone? Where were the hopes with which he'd been born? Where was his birthright of innocence now? He'd not spent it—and that was for sure. Yet here he was, Nicholas Kemp, scarce two and twenty, an outcast and a scapegoat, damned if ever a man was—even waiting to be hanged. He'd a glum notion that, though many a naked beggar got into Heaven, gentlemen who wore cravats of rope were most likely directed elsewhere . . .

Suddenly, the rhythm of the chains was disturbed. The regular tolling was changed into a rapid clatter. Likewise, the heaving motion of the ship (which, in the extreme darkness, Nicholas was profoundly sensitive to) altered to a curious shuddering.

On deck, the helmsman struggled with the wheel, for the *Phoenix* was come upon one of the strong submarine currents whose presence, in sunlight, proclaims itself in long, glass-smooth fingers stretched across the rippled sea. The effect was as if some profound monster was wrenching at the ship's keel.

The entire passage across this current lasted maybe no

more than seven or eight minutes, but such was the loudness and violence of the shaking irons that Nicholas was all but deafened. When it stopped, and the old beating was resumed, he could hear nothing external for several minutes, and mistook an urgent knocking for his own blood banging in his head.

"Sonny! Sonny—are you there? Answer me, boy! It's Bartleman here! Speak up if you're still alive!"

Amazed out of his misery, Nicholas cried out, "Is it you? Is it really you?"

Bartleman laughed—and there was no mistaking the sound of it.

"It's really me, sonny. Ain't that a fine thing to hear in the dark?"

"You've no idea, Mister Bartleman! No idea at all how fine it is! Where are you?"

"Behind the bulkhead, sonny. Had you forgot? We're all here. Tell this poor, unhappy lad you're all here! Let him hear your voices!"

Directly, came a score of voices, low but thick with affection, wishing him well and urging him keep in good heart.

"That's enough!" ordered Bartleman. "Quiet, now. Time enough for roaring later. Eh? Eh?"

Nicholas's spirits began to flicker and to rise. If ever

he'd suspected the embezzler's kindness (which he never had), such suspicions would now have been truly laid. Fierce and violent as was that man, there was a heart in him such as few possessed. There was some good in the world after all—be it never so oddly lodged.

"They'll not hang you, sonny."

"Much thanks for your comfort, Mister Bartleman, but I think they will."

"No contradictions, sonny. When Bartleman says they won't, they won't. For it's not Bartleman alone. There's eighty downtrodden gentlemen here who says the same. Ain't that so, gentlemen?"

Came a dark chorus of agreement—most determined; most formidable.

"Did you hear that powerful eighty, sonny? Each and every one of 'em feels it would be right villainous to hang a gentle, simple soul like you. And will put his feelings into action—without which feelings is so much trash!" (Here, the embezzler's voice took on a cutting edge.) "D'you take my meaning, sonny?"

"The ship? You'll take over the ship, Mister Bartleman? D'you mean mutiny, sir?"

Nicholas's spirits began to dive and twist and whirl—as might a leaf or a fledgling caught in a sudden crosswind. The sensible part of his mind assured him that Mr.

Bartleman was but trying to comfort him in his last hours by filling them with hope: but another part of his mind provoked an unnatural excitement . . .

"Call it what you like, sonny. For my part, I'll call it the terrible meek in'eriting a little bit of the earth. Or a rising up, sonny, on be'alf of you. Or, if you like, a rightchus anger for the poor little bleeding oppressed. Take your pick, son—it's six of one and half a dozen of the other. All that matters is that you can sleep easy, sonny. Bartleman's a-watching over you."

He did sleep—but not easily. His soul was much torn with excitement and uneasiness and a gloomy conviction that he'd have no more luck in escaping the hangman's rope than he'd had in what was gruesomely known as love.

"Love!" murmured Nicholas, dreamily. "You've broke my heart, and now you'll break my neck."

Then, little by little, his old nature asserted itself and hope came creeping back. Bartleman, the embezzler— whose voice he could hear murmuring from time to time on the other side of the bulkhead—would not let poor Nick Kemp die. He had promised. Bartleman would—

"Thank you, Mister Bartleman," he murmured before he dozed off. "You are indeed my good angel . . ."

And when he awoke, his eyes were wet with tears . . .

· 5 ·

Having nothing of black in her luggage but half a yard of lace of her mother's, Miss Warboys slept badly and woke early, still wondering whether to wear it at her throat or on her hair. But her reddened eyes and stained cheeks—though she'd never have declared it—had a deeper cause than vanity over a touch of mourning. Her heart ached: gentle Mr. Kemp had stolen more than a brooch . . .

But nothing was ever decided by sighing. The lace became her reddish hair distractingly well—and three pins would hold it if the air proved kind. It all depended on the weather. Anxiously, she rouged the tearstains out of her cheeks and stumbled forth to see how strong the wind blew.

The morning was palely brilliant. The eastern sea seemed to have washed all the blood out of the sun so that it hung over the poop like a glaring ghost.

The air was cold but had little motion. Most likely this was on account of all sails being furled—which gave the ship an open aspect, as of a house suddenly unroofed.

There was no doubt that three pins would secure the black lace quite confidently.

"I must look well for him," she murmured, clinging to her pertness though her passions were in disarray. "I must look my —Oh God—God! How horrible!"

From the larboard arm of the mainyard hung a rope that was no part of the rigging.

"Hemp for Kemp, miss," said the boatswain, harshly; then laid his hands behind his back and stared down at the hatch that covered the thief to die.

Though the rope appalled her, she could not forebear from looking at it again and again before she returned to her quarters.

Nor was she alone in this. The merciful Captain had seen it with displeasure and even with pain. For he *was* a merciful man—though cursed with a quick temper and a loose tongue. It was certain he regretted the sudden sentence he'd passed in the night. But his word was law to the boatswain, and laws must be kept else they fall into disrepute and are booted aside.

If I weaken now, he thought fiercely, them thieving felons will have the gold out of me passengers' teeth! No! Examples must be made—then we can all rest easy.

"Boatswain!" he shouted from the quarter-deck—and in the general stillness, his voice ranged high and wide— "I want everything done shipshape! Crew on the forecastle

head. Convicts in their enclosure. No passengers near 'em. I'll have no more thievery! They can keep to their cabins or come out with me. Shipshape. D'you understand?"

"Aye, Captain. Shall I read the service?"

"That's my office, mister. You can dispatch him, but I'll address him. Get moving, mister. And do it neat and decent. Remember—there'll be ladies present."

The boatswain moved. Put into motion the Captain's orders. Eased out the crew from every dozy cranny and dicing hole. Crossed and recrossed the staring deck. A hard and vigilant man.

Sourly, the Captain watched, then returned to his cabin to ferret out his Bible. On his way, he remembered the paying passengers. He frowned. Had brief hopes of their keeping to the Great Cabin till the—the unpleasantness was done with.

His hopes were dashed when he saw them, warmly dressed and full of expectation . . .

"Gentlemen and ladies," he said irritably. "I must ask you to keep well aft, poopward, I mean, of the mainmast this morning. An—an example is being made. For the convicts. It—it really ain't your business. Begging your pardon! It ain't interesting. But of course, if you insists . . . Gentlemen—I'll trouble you to look to the ladies. Some turns queasy. I recommend aromatic vinegar—Miss Warboys! It won't do no good, y'know—not to him nor to you, miss. It wasn't your fault . . . and you won't make it any easier on him. Better for him to think on spiritual matters when—Miss Warboys! Bear up, my girl!"

This last, as Miss Warboys tottered and clutched at the table for support. She recovered herself, attempted one of her smiles (which seemed to pluck at her lips like a child begging), then felt for the piece of black lace that lay atop her head.

"Saucy slut!" remarked a female passenger, and Miss Warboys's eyes glittered with a touch of anger.

"Did you see? Did you mark? *That* went home!"

The sun was halfway up the mizzen—a blinding eye to stare the world out of countenance. There was no looking backward toward it . . .

The masts flung terrible great shadows the length of the deck. These shadows were wide and thick like velvet, and lay most ominously across the hatch that covered up Nicholas Kemp.

"Boatswain!" shouted the Captain.

"Sir?"

"All assembled?"

"Aye, sir."

"Then let up the convicts first. Open up their hatch. Move, man!"

Came a curious effect. The mainmast's shadow lay three quarters across this hatch, so that the Captain shouted a second time before he saw the shabby felons spilling over the edge of the blackness and understood the shadow to be hiding them as they emerged.

Now a slight wind sprang up, coming from the northwest. The flat sea prickled and the *Phoenix* began, very gently, to dance.

"Get 'em moving, mister! Quicker, there!"

The Captain most likely feared the wind would increase and blow his sermon too early to Heaven.

"Move, you stinking felons!" roared the boatswain. "Else you'll all end up with Kemp!"

But the convicts did not seem to hurry themselves. And rather than from the angry boatswain, they seemed to take direction from a squat convict who shifted deftly in and out of the mainmast's shadow, so that one moment he was plainly seen, and the next there was nothing but an invisible presence, somewhere in the dark.

"Are they all come up yet?"

"I'll go see, sir. I think—ah!"

The boatswain had gone into the dark, toward the invisible presence.

"What's amiss, there? What are they doing? Boatswain! Damn you, mister! Answer me or—"

But if that vigilant man had been damned, it was now by a powerfuller Judge than the *Phoenix*'s Captain. He lay in the black shadow, dead of Bartleman's knife.

There followed now movement and purpose of uncanny speed and skill—which the very brilliance of the day obscured.

Even as a shoal of black perch in a summer's stream may twist and dart and vanish utterly in the shadows of overhanging leaves and branches, so the rapid dark figures of the running convicts vanished in the deep, wide shadow of the mainmast. Nothing was seen—but there was heard the terrible sound of their tread, under which the deck trembled . . .

Wild confusion had broken out on the forecastle head! But the man who might have quelled and commanded it was shrewdly dead. Muskets were swung and desperately leveled—But against what? Valuable moments lost; moments that were now beyond price.

Already this dark and pounding army was swarming out of its concealment and overrunning the quarter-deck. Already the Captain was overthrown. Muskets shook and trembled—but the damnable sun glared too bright for a certain aim. It was too late—and the ruined Captain knew it.

"Don't shoot! For pity's sake, don't shoot, men! Remember—for God's sake remember, there's ladies present!"

The embezzler, profiting as he always did by softer natures than his own, had directed the passengers to be seized and held in the path of any presumptuous musketry. His own squat person he shielded with the unlucky Miss Warboys—holding his stained knife to that trembling side of her that was best in the Captain's view.

"Disarm 'em, friend—or this poor innocent soul dies for it. Come now, friend—would you want her death at your door?"

He'd a way of saying "innocent" (a favorite word of his) so that it seemed bent in the middle and robbed of meaning.

Wretchedly, the Captain stared at the grinning embezzler. There was no mistaking his intent, nor belittling his power to carry it out.

"Throw down them muskets!" he shouted, but his voice was so unsteady with anger, fear, and grief that he had to shout again and again before the crew on the forecastle head heard him plain enough to obey. Then several of the convicts ran forward and gathered up the weapons in a triumph they themselves could scarce believe in.

Maybe five minutes had been needed since they'd come out of their hold and into the iron sunlight for them to possess the ship that had been their prison. To the best and worst of their understanding, they were free!

Five minutes. Each and every one of them had been counted out by Nicholas Kemp. Each sound, each cry, each rumble of feet on the deck above had been translated a thousand ways in his eager mind—till there came the shout and roar that Mr. Bartleman had promised. They were free! The shadow of death lifted. Any instant now the hatch would be moved and friends would come climbing down—

Convicts were ransacking the passengers' quarters. Bartleman had given them leave. ("Enjoy yourselves, sons!") Roar upon roar of happy triumph declared their finds . . . while the passengers trembled in the verminous grip of felons whose turn was still to come.

"There weren't no harshness—no cruelty—" moaned the Captain, more to himself than to the raucous gentry who reeked about his quarter-deck.

Shrieks of laughter came suddenly out of the poop. A party of mad propriety had come falling out. The convicts had got at the passengers' baggage. Had decked themselves to the eyeballs in genteel attire. Pantaloons and waistcoats being bespoke, they'd sorted out hooped gowns and solemn petticoats, bombazeen bodices and hats like birds of prey. Arm in arm, they hopped and capered, kicking up their feet which emerged from under daintiness like huge black insects uncovered at a garden feast.

In fatherly fashion, Bartleman watched them; laughed, made jokes, seemed affable, at ease . . . as if with all the time in the world . . .

In the darkness of his jail, Nicholas Kemp made excuses for the delay. Much had to be accomplished; the crew shut up, the mutiny secured. First things first—and then they'd come . . .

On the wild and violent deck, the unlucky Captain groaned, "Why? Why?" over and over—as if the certain death he read in the embezzler's eyes would be eased by knowing the reason for it.

"A good question, friend," answered Bartleman, obligingly. He was in high good humor over the antics of his men which continually diverted him—as if underneath all his terrible implacability was a mass of merriment that could not help breaking through. "You was going to hang a man—Ha! Look at that!" (Something fresh had amused him. God knew what!) "A meek, oppressed young soul. So we rose up on his be'alf. Rose up in our wrath. Rage of the downtrodden, you might call it, friend. The anger of the weak and 'elpless, so to speak. Ha! What a sight! Don't it tickle the ribs and warm the heart, friend?" (But the Captain's blood stayed cold as ice.) "You might even say—if you'd a mind to—the poor meek has in'erited this small piece of the earth, friend. Take your pick. It's six of one or half a dozen of the other. It's all because you was going to hang poor Nick Kemp."

All this delivered with an affable air over the shoulder of Miss Warboys. On the mention of Nick Kemp, her deathly face took on some faint color and she began to moan and struggle till Bartleman pricked her side with his knife and made her cry out—

"Kemp?" screamed the Captain. "For Kemp? Then for God's sake, free him! I give in! He's pardoned! You've won your cause! Take him up! All's forgiven! Not a word'll be said hereafter! I promise—on my honor—"

"What was that you said, friend?"

Abruptly, the Captain gave up his pleading. All urgency was pricked; all hope sunk. Bleakly he stared in the embezzler's face which was gone suddenly bland. He understood too well that Nicholas Kemp was no more than the martyr whose only purpose was to make the fire burn bright. Bitterly, he cursed him for the meekness that had fed this monster's strength.

"Damn you, Kemp! Damn you for unlocking this Hell!"

In the darkness below, Nicholas Kemp fancied he heard—above the uproar that went with the convicts' liberty—his name called out. Cheerfully, he shouted back, "I'm here, gentlemen! Much thanks for all you've done!" And he stared up to the hatch, with all his amiable young soul fixed on the expectation of its opening any moment now.

On the quarter-deck, one of the ship's officers, in mad and valiant mood, fancied his chances with the squat, vulgar little convict before whom his Captain shrank.

"Come along, man. Give up this madness. Kemp won't thank you—"

Still in chains, Nicholas Kemp waited. Then he heard a scream, and Mr. Bartleman shout, "For Kemp! That was for Kemp!"

What was for him? Another man's life. The scream had a rasp of mortality to it. A sudden and horrible agony invaded the young man, like a blast of winter through his vitals. Into what dark sea had he been led—and there to drown? What business had he in the world that men should die for him? He stared up at the hatch—but now with fading hope . . . and even with dread.

The ship began to rock more violently, for the wind was increasing. Nicholas began to be toppled from side to side, to the extent of his chain. Then, with appalling suddenness, a fresh disaster struck.

On deck, the ship's motion had brought an almost tipsy gaiety to the convicts. Crazy preparations were afoot for dispatching the passengers with dreadful entertainment —when a frightful sound halted them. Directly, faces grew pale with uneasy questioning, as if the sound was of some supernatural vengeance.

It came from below. It was loud and regular. A formidable rumbling, like fallen thunder, cut off at each extremity by a loud crash. And then there came up, from the same dark place, a frantic cry, "Help me! Help me! The irons have got loose! I'll be crushed to death!"

"Save him!" shrieked Miss Warboys, careless of the twice-red knife—

But Bartleman the embezzler grinned in huge delight, as if the merriment inside of him had finally burst its bounds. He could scarce contain his laughter in the mounting wind.

"Crushed to death! Poor Kemp!" he roared. "Now

we've sanctified this mutiny in an innocent's blood! We got the right, sons! Oh yes, we got the right! We dedicate this freedom to the soul of poor Nick Kemp! And don't no one go down to fish him out and spoil it!"

Now the wind blew a fierce, malicious blast. But Miss Warboys was long way past caring—even though her half yard of lace was whipped from her head and fluttered wildly in the air like a long-darkened soul taking wing . . .

· 6 ·

The gnawing of the rats, the violent shaking caused by passage across the submarine current and now the sudden springing up of the wind, had together broken a securing rope. Thus some dozen of heavy leg irons flew and crashed from side to side with malignant force.

The effect of this, in the extreme darkness, was at once extraordinary and terrible.

If ever a living soul had knowledge of the whirlwinds of Hell, then that soul belonged to the young man chained to the mainmast.

With no liberty but that offered by four feet of chain, and no warning of each onslaught save by terrified listen-

ing, he must needs crouch and leap—he knew not where
—as the invisible irons came rushing past.

Sometimes, these leaps were too vigorous, and then he
was brought down, with painful reminder, by his chain.
But not to rest. Even as he lay, conceiving his fettered leg
to be broken and his head in ruins, he heard the onslaught
begin again. Out of each echoing crash it came—a harsh
screaming as the iron rasped across the boards, growing
louder and louder and infecting him with desperation
to escape if only for seconds more.

Faintly, from above, he could hear the shouts and sometime laughter of the convicts who owned the ship. But
such sounds no longer moved him. Plainly, from above, he
had heard Bartleman shout. He had heard himself contemptuously dedicated to death.

He leaped sideways, and felt the wind of something
passing. Then he lay still for seconds while Bartleman's
words burned in his brain as if that gentle space so full
of springtime love and springtime hope was changed into
a crucible . . .

Now he imagined the squat embezzler standing in the
dark, hurling the irons at him—

"I've come for your soul, sonny!"

"Not this time . . . not this time!"

"I've paid for it, sonny, with a pipe!"

"That wasn't for my soul . . . not my soul!"

"I paid for it with the Marshalsea man's life, sonny!"

"That wasn't for my soul—"

"I paid for it with a brooch, sonny, and with a fair face. *That* was for your soul!"

Each of these exchanges marked a thundering past of the irons, and a desperate escape from them, though each escape grew more hazardous as the young man tired.

"Not for my soul . . ."

"You took the brooch and bought Miss Warboys's love—"

"I gave—I gave! I bought nothing! I gave her my soul! You can't have it, Bartleman! It's not here! It's not mine! I've beaten you, Bartleman—you've only embezzled yourself!"

"It's too late, sonny, too late!"

Again the irons thundered; again Nicholas leaped—but weariness and deafening confusion caused him to be deceived in the sound. He leaped backward. And it was the mainmast alone that saved him. A most terrific conglomeration of iron struck and lodged against his leg. Though its chief force was spent upon the mast, a stray pendant almost broke his knee.

"Next time your soul, sonny," the imaginary Bartleman seemed to say. "Next time, eh?"

Now the next time was on its way, rumbling in the darkness . . .

Nicholas made to move. Demons had been at work on his knee, most likely with something white hot. But there was worse than that, even. His own chain had been entangled, caught up in the iron. From four feet of liberty, he'd scarce a foot remaining.

He shouted aloud in a rage that was tragic and pitiful, for here indeed was the rage of the meek, tricked out of inheritance and seeking redress in the Court of Heaven. Then the invisible creatures (whose shapes were now in his mind grimacing devils and savage beasts) rushed roaring by and met the opposing woodwork with a very doom-laden sound.

He began to feel for the entanglement. Not much time could be left to him. Chain upon chain seemed to meet his frantic fingers. The knot was dense—immovable. He felt further, heedless of loss of skin and nails. Indeed, the pain seemed to give him a curious courage and strength . . .

The leg iron that had struck him was one of the old sort. It consisted, he discovered, of two bars of metal which—in happier circumstances—would be fastened at one extremity to ankles, and at the other, to a chain fixed about the waist. But now one of these bars was lodged between the bolthead in the mast and the linkage of Nicholas's chain. Not even the smith who made them could have devised a more ingenious use nor a stricter hold upon their victim.

The ship tilted and the thundering began again. Above, he heard fresh shouting that marked some new event—or the cheerful expectancy of it. Then the roaring grew deafening as the irons rushed in a changed direction.

He believed he felt the air shift hurriedly as they came at him—even as if some living creature had puffed its breath into his face.

"God have mercy on me!" he shrieked—and pulled with such strength and desperation as he never knew he had. Then the irons struck.

For a moment, he believed his leg was gone. He cursed and groaned as he flew through the dark, to thump most painfully against a bulkhead.

But he was whole. He was whole and free and healthy —or as much so as any man might be, half dead with pain and terror, with four feet of chain fixed to his ankle, and lost in a darkness that was filled with the roaring of loose irons.

When the irons had struck, they had met the entangling bar with extraordinary force; which force, thus invested in leverage, had yielded high profit. It had wrenched the bolthead from the mast. Fetters had freed Nicholas Kemp from fetters.

The murder of the passengers had been delayed by rea-son of the need to put out a drift anchor—the sea running high and the *Phoenix* tossing with much distraction.

Four of the crew had accomplished this, either from hopes of saving themselves or from a pride in their calling which would not suffer them to let a ship go down even though they themselves might not live to see it sail.

Yet such was the scene on deck that it might have been better for the sea to engulf it than expose it to the strong light of the sun.

On the quarter-deck, the passengers were kneeling at their prayers, for to each and all of them, it had been made abundantly plain that they were not, any of them, long for this world. So they said their prayers, with many a topple sideways as the ship pitched. As they struggled to recover (being quaintly concerned that God might think ill of them if they didn't make the effort), Bartleman would give them a humorous push, to see them topple again.

He was in an extraordinarily good humor, and seemed to draw strength from the very air. He could not stop himself from grinning, and his breathing sounded like laughter.

Was he mad, then? Hard to say. If compassion, kindness, and humanity are the qualities of sanity, then Bartleman was mad, for he possessed none of them. And, being mad, he had the strength of ten.

"Justice!" he shouted. "In the name of justice and to the memory of poor Nick Kemp! Heave away, there!"

The unhappy Captain stood upon the bulwark below the mainyard. The rope he himself had ordered was fastened round his own neck.

"Heave away!" repeated Bartleman, with a touch of peevishness that the Captain wasn't swinging and kicking directly.

But the convicts who'd been awarded the office still failed to heave. Their attention was elsewhere. It was upon a hatch.

Bartleman scowled. Terrible sight. But even yet the hatch took more attention. Now the crew stared at it; now the passengers rose from their knees. Miss Warboys lifted her head from her hands; and the Captain turned, quite forgetful of the strangling rope.

What was there about the hatch that diminished Bartleman? It was moving. It rose—and fell . . . then rose again. Monstrous effort from beneath. It groaned, wood against wood, but heavy as stone on stone. It began to slide . . . farther and farther—Then the deck tilted generously—and the hatch was gone!

A groan of amazement filled the air. A frightful sight was emerging. Slowly and painfully, with much grimacing . . .

Battered about the head, filthy, bleeding, hands and

fingers of no more consequence than ragged gloves, even with four feet of chain still hanging to one ankle, rose up Nicholas Kemp.

"Well, sonny!" shouted Bartleman savagely. "Come back from the dead, have you?"

"Yes," answered Nicholas. "I left something behind."

"Indeed you did?"

"Indeed I did. I left you, Bartleman. I've come back to fetch you."

By the terror in which he was beheld, it was plain that many thought—for some moments—that Nick Kemp was indeed dead and returned. For his emerging was uncanny and his aspect changed as if by passage through the grave. There was almost a supernatural sternness in his eyes, as if he was become the representative of all the meek, the foolish, the obliging, and the gentle whose name and whose cause had ever been taken in vain. In every heart save one, his aspect struck an old familiar chord.

But not in Bartleman's. *He* was never so deceived. Rather was he violently angry at this—this specter at his feast.

"So you want a word with me, sonny?"

Of a sudden, something like his old fears clutched at Nicholas's heart. The embezzler, though squat and with a seeming short reach, was a compact of venomous deftness and power. He lacked doubt; he lacked gentleness—which two qualities Nicholas owned in full measure.

Confused, Nicholas stared about him. In patches still, the sun was blinding and hurt his eyes. He gazed along the quarter-deck. He saw Miss Warboys—who returned his gaze with a smile that, by reason of its very frailty, seemed at that moment to be the strongest thing on earth. It gave him heart . . . even though, at that moment, heart was not what he chiefly needed. A pistol would have been more to the purpose.

Bartleman had come down. Bartleman was standing, three yards off, legs apart, nodding and grinning.

"Can't say I'm not polite, sonny. That word you wanted. I've come to collect it."

Gently, he swung his knife.

So Nicholas began to move. The embezzler watched with interest. The childish simpleton moved somewhat more deftly than he'd have supposed . . . considering he'd to drag his four feet of chain and wrenched-out bolt behind him. Pitiful fellow . . . pitiful . . .

A curious lightness seemed to possess Nicholas. Most likely, this was following on his heavy struggle below. The chain seemed no more than gossamer, and followed on like a shadow. Also, to see his enemy, formidable though he was, gave him an easiness and space to contrive

. . . which had not been so below, when he'd fought with the monsters of the dark.

Thus it was almost without interest that he saw the passengers and crew watching him with hope and pity. While the convicts, of a sudden, seemed to him no more fierce or purposeful than sheep on a hillside, watching without understanding while a wolf and a dog were about to fight for their lives. For a moment, this thought oppressed him dangerously; then he saw Miss Warboys and at once understood that he had no business to lack interest.

"I'm a-waiting, sonny. I'm a-waiting for you, lad."

With dismay, Nicholas realized what he was about. It was as if the terrible Bartleman had ordered him . . . for he was circling helplessly—even as the Marshalsea man had done before him.

Wildly, he halted. Bartleman smiled—and took two paces toward him.

"Sorry—but I'm in a trifle of a hurry, sonny."

Again, Nicholas began to move. Bartleman watched him round. The distance between them was fatally shrunk.

What advantage now in the light of the day? The monsters of the dark had taught him nothing—save the weight and power of iron. And what had he learned from the dark itself? Nothing—save that the sun was blinding bright.

Where was the sun now? Still over the poop. It had not fallen from the sky. Amazing. It shone with appalling brilliance on Bartleman's face whenever he faced aft, turning his eyes to spots of fire.

But now, with a quickening heart, Nicholas made a discovery. No more than a trifle; a feather, almost, that came floating down to weight the scales in which his life was cradled. What was this trifle, then? A hurrying in the embezzler's movements whenever he faced aft, and briefly, thereafter, an uncertain slowing down. It was as if he'd seen a second Nicholas Kemp, loitering after the first . . . Then he'd recover himself and resume his relentless watch. Till he faced the sun again . . .

The sun was blinding him, printing false images on his eye! Now with increasing speed, Nicholas moved about Bartleman—save whenever he passed the poop. And then he dragged almost to a halt.

But implacably, Bartleman kept pace. Even glared monstrously into the very eye of Heaven when it was on him . . . so strong of purpose was this man. But his very strength was his weakness—even as Nick Kemp's weakness was now his strength, his heart being neither in his boots nor in his mouth but on the poopdeck with Miss Warboys and out of his present keeping.

Now Bartleman began to falter—then straightened

again. Grinned and followed, with horribly inflamed eyes . . . followed the image of a Nick Kemp that the sun had burned upon his brain.

So it's possible that he never saw the rush that was made upon him when he faced the poop for the last time. He must have heard it—heard the four feet of chain and wrenched-off bolt clink and bang and dance across the deck, but he moved awry. Seemed to plunge, knife deftly glittering, toward a simpleton made of air. And, meeting no resistance, he began to fall—

"A word!" he cried. "Best be—"

Then he gave a most pitiful grunt, such as an ox or a pig might give when its day is done. His fall was finished. He would fall no more; nor would ever rise.

Like an avenging lash, the iron bolt and chain from Nicholas's ankle had whirled through the air and struck him in the neck. Amazed, the young man turned to look for his enemy. But Bartleman was dead. His neck had been broken like a discarded pipe . . .

The mutiny was ended. The heart and mind of the corporate beast lay ruined before its eyes. For a moment, a profound dismay seized the convicts, then this changed to wonderment—and then to a strange relief as they saw the ragged and oddly frail young man stare with a kind of startled sadness at what he'd done.

There was a brief and confused notion of offering him the vacant leadership . . . for they were none of them Bartleman. But it was plain he would not have it. Content he might be to take the fruits of victory—he did not want the tree. Such power as was, of necessity, momentarily his, he used to restore the Captain to his office and all else to theirs. True, a few men grumbled, a few men looked askance, a few men even loitered on a violent hope. But there were none of them who'd damn himself to try to catch the universal fear. They were—when all was said and done—more gentlemen of ill fortune than men of ill will.

And now a storm of cheerfulness burst over the ship and the shadow of damnation was blown to the winds. The paying passengers dipped into their hearts and gave three cheers for Nicholas Kemp; likewise, the crew. Then, when the echoes had died, the convicts begged leave to try their voices, too. And their cheers were longest and loudest of all, for they knew, better than any, what was demanded of a man to outface the murderous Mr. Bartleman.

But what of the hero now? He had been led up upon the quarter-deck where, despite the powerful smells that came off of him, his back was thumped and his hand was wrung and every man counted himself honored to honor him. Yet he stared at the multitude of faces and heard the multitude of voices as if in a dream. Then he covered his face with his hands . . . and when he took them away, it was plainly seen that he was weeping.

"For God's sake, why?" shouted the Captain, thumping him again and again on the back, as if to give him something to cry about. "A prize! A prize! A cash prize, Master Kemp! That's what you'll get!"

Indeed, the Captain seemed to have got cash, prizes, and Master Kemp on the brain, and showed every sign of staying so demented till his mania should come true. He was inclined to hop and dance about a good deal, often twisting his head abruptly—as if to reassure himself the rope was gone. Then he'd scrutinize the shadows—now much shrunk, for the sun was high—nod and gaze upward to the yards, the fitful sails, the topmasts and the pennants. On which he'd beam and wipe his brow, as if he'd been auditing his blessings and found himself to be in credit . . . when his mania would assert itself again and he'd insist, "Ten thousand pounds, I shouldn't wonder! Value of the ship! And more! A cash prize, Master Kemp! God save you!"

Then he bethought himself further. "And your freedom as well! I promise! Think of it—freedom and a cash prize, my boy!"

In vain, the bewildered young man tried to think of it, but his mind had a mind of its own. Either he'd lost his wits (as the Captain suspected), or he could not help thinking of other things.

Suddenly, there was a touch on his arm whose very lightness, in contrast to past powerful honorings, arrested him. He turned. Beside him stood Miss Warboys.

His knees shook, his heart beat fast, and under the bruises and filth, a blush overspread his face. She smiled somewhat timidly at him, and a female passenger said, "Ah!"

Wonderingly, he looked down on his battlefield, then back to the lady. Was *she* the cause of his victory? Was it no more than this red-haired young woman whose reddened eyes winked and shone with an ocean of soft tears?

No *more* than? Was it not enough then? Was there anybody on board the *Phoenix* that day who doubted that it was enough? For where else can lie the strength of the gentle and the meek save in love?

"A favor, Captain," murmured Nicholas, uncertainly. "Might I beg a favor, sir?"

"A favor?" declared the Captain, astonished to the world. "He begs a favor? Freedom and a cash prize, my boy! Don't you understand? It's all yours!" (He paused to glance reassuringly into the shadows.) "All right— what's the favor, then? Out with it! A hundred pounds in advance? Ha-ha! We can manage. It's yours!"

Suddenly, he observed Nicholas's arm clasping Miss Warboys about the waist. He smiled; he beamed; he began to laugh and rub his hands together.

"Me Bible!" he cried. "Me Good Book! I knew there'd be a use for it. I take it you want me to exercise me office, Master Kemp?"

Vigorously, Nicholas Kemp nodded. Out of all proportion to the circumstance in hand was his relief that he'd been spared making his own proposal.

She made a charming bride—there on the quarter-deck. It was on the very next morning, which was Sunday, January 31. Two bridesmaids had Caroline Warboys— which was more than she'd dreamed of when she'd set sail. And the tears shed by the female passengers were enough to have floated a longboat.

"Ain't she a picture?" sobbed one. "The sweet and happy darling!"

In March of the year 1750, the *Phoenix* (now on her last voyage) sailed into the Potomac River in Virginia, with a cargo of hinges for pine furniture, muslins, silks, and thirty convicted felons.

Among these latter were three young men of good families who had been sentenced—at Lewes Assizes—to seven years' transportation for being in possession of stolen property.

On the quayside, they drew a great deal of attention to themselves by loudly protesting that they'd been ill used, unjustly sentenced, and that money would be coming from England to purchase their bonds.

They continued in this manner for some time, arrogantly ignoring the auctioning of their bonds as if birth and breeding took precedence over law and Fate.

They fetched very little, being of a worthless and puny appearance . . . somewhat sickly and spotted on the nose and cheeks—as if they'd drunk too many healths for the good of their own.

But appearances can be very deceptive. Indeed, their purchaser got quite a bargain in them, and—despite his being a new owner, having purchased his plantation with a cash prize in the preceding year—was ever after looked up to as a remarkably shrewd judge.

He got seven of the hardest years' work out of those three well-born young men that the settlement could ever remember. They became almost proverbial while they were at it, and often were held up as an example of industry and a desire to atone for their sins.

Be that as it may, their ceaseless labors did much to increase their owner's prosperity, so that there might well have been some truth in the rumor that they'd once been acquainted with him in England.

Had that indeed been so, and that there'd been some arrears of friendship between them, there's no doubt that they paid off their debt in full. If Trojans had worked as they did, in all weathers, then Troy would never have fallen. Certainly, friendship must have been at the root of it all; for there never was a man so blessed in his friends as dear, amiable Nick Kemp . . .